A Man's Passion

JERRY SCHELLHAMMER

A MAN'S PASSION

ISBN (Paperback): 979-8-89672-206-9
ISBN (Ebook): 979-8-89672-207-6

Printed in the United States of America.

PROMINENT
BOOKS
EDGE

5830 E 2nd St, Ste 7000 #9983
Casper, WY 82609
USA

PROLOGUE

Earlier in the day, two men stole a truck from a county prison gang and ended up near Americus and this Walmart. The truck was a 2000 Dodge Ram 2500 with a crew cab. They were dressed in white and black prison uniforms and at two in the morning, only a few employees bothered to take notice when they went inside. The surveillance cameras caught everything though.

They went to the clothesline and picked their choice of denim jeans, t- shirts that advertised their favorite brand of beer, a pair of Atlanta Braves baseball caps and found two pairs of Air Jordans. They went into the fitting room and changed their clothes. They then raced out of the store before the employees noticed, but the alarms alerted them the moment the two sprinted out of the entrance. Though several employees scrambled after them, Spike and Rufus drove out the parking lot and were on US 280 and heading toward Columbus, Georgia.

DOT & HATTIE

"Granny Hattie, are you ready?" Hattie Black looked across the small room of her dorm. She smiled at her great-granddaughter through cat-eyed framed bi-focal glasses, her back appeared stooped, the wrinkles on her pale, ivory face pronounced, and the liver spotted hands that held her walker in front used most all the time anymore to help her to maneuver about the assisted living facility.

Dorothy, though everyone in their family called her Dot, just turned twenty and was engaged to a college football athlete named Rex. Dot's nose piercing gave away her generation, along with the tattoo of a unicorn prominently displayed on her upper back and shoulder, to the chagrin of her great grandmother. Her brown hair had a natural curl to it. Dot wore white shorts, white blouse and sandals, her Ray Bans held up on her head.

Hattie Black used her walker to pull herself up from the twin sized hospital bed. She lived in Coral Gables, Florida. Her Georgia accent ran from her mouth as smooth as molasses. "Soon child soon," she replied as she moved slowly in the direction of her front door. "Dot, where are we going again?" She smiled broadly at her great granddaughter.

"Montgomery, Alabama. Remember? You wanted to go to that lynching museum.

"And I told you I would drive you there," Dot replied pulling her sunglasses over her brown eyes. She sounded stressed and frustrated by always reminding her great grandmother of things she wanted to do but seemingly, increasingly, always forgetting.

"I read in the newspaper a police officer shot another Black boy."

"Yes, ma'am, but they prefer we call them African American now." Hattie smiled at her.

"Not so long ago, child, my Pa used another word. He used it regular as clockwork." Dot frowned. "And he would have called you an Oriol."

"Did he live to see what happened?"

"Oh yes, he did. I hoped he would have changed over time, but he didn't. I sure do hope he's resting comfortably in that oak casket of his."

"Are you gonna talk about all that time on the way to Montgomery?"

Hattie's azure eyes looked deep into her great granddaughter's before she replied, "In time child in time."

Dot grabbed Hattie's cane made of oak too and handed it to her. "You can leave that thing here." She left the walker just inside the door and secured the door firmly. She held Hattie's left hand, while Hattie's right hand grasped the cane, and they began walking toward the main lobby in a slow and steady gait. The reception nurse, Miss Georgia sat and waved at them with her large, fat hands. Her cocoa- colored face radiated with a smile as she saw the pair leave the retirement center.

"Y'all bring Hattie back in one piece now. She's got her 100th birthday coming next week," Miss Georgia called out to Dot.

"I'll tan her hide if she doesn't," Hattie called out in reply, which garnered a laugh from the nurse.

Out front sat Dot's 2003 Toyota Prius. It was black with a hatchback and Hattie right away didn't appreciate it. "That's a small car Dot. You sure it's gonna make it all the way to Alabama?"

Dot crinkled her nose in bemusement. "Granny Hat, I'll have you know, I've been all over the south in this car going to job interviews for when I get out of college next spring." Her naturally tanned face took on a redder hue of anger at her great grandmother.

"It's a Toyota too," Hattie criticized. "You all wouldn't be doing that knowing the sacrifice your Great grandpa Black made, along with my brother Billy. You kids these days don't remember but I do!"

"I wasn't there!" Dot cried out in frustration, throwing her hands in the air. She suddenly saw the hurt expression of Hattie's quivering mouth. "I'm sorry Grandma Hattie. I'll tell you what, the first car I get from the first job offered me, I'll buy me an American made car, like a Ford or Dodge…"

"Oldsmobile," Hattie interrupted her. "What was that ma'am?"

"I want it to be an Oldsmobile."

"But they ain't been made since 2000!"

"That's fine, child. I guess I'm ready." She slowly placed herself inside the car, ensuring the cane came in last before firmly closing the car door. Dot got behind the wheel, pressed a button to engage the engine and placed the shifter into drive. They left together for the National Memorial for Peace and Justice.

"Child, how far is it to Montgomery?" "Let's see Grandma Hattie." While driving in downtown Coral

Gables traffic, she pulled out her smartphone and did a Google search.

"What in tarnation are you doing Dorothy Mae Black?"

"It's fine Grandma Hattie. I do it all the time."

"You pull off this street right now and park this car. Then you do that!"

She rolled her eyes, though Hattie couldn't see it and pulled into a Wal mart parking lot. "Okay it says here; 681 miles and we'll get there in over ten hours."

"We'll have to stay the night in a Travel Lodge. Ain't no way this old body can go that far anymore."

"Yes, ma'am, we'll find us a place in Georgia before concluding in Montgomery."

Hattie tried to relax on the bucket seats, though it seemed an effort. She moved this way and that. She found the seat adjust lever and it went forward, then back. "Tarnation, girl this car has a curse against me. I can't seem to get comfortable, Dot."

"Oh Grandma! Just try and find a proper adjustment on that seat."

"I'm trying, darling. Oh, here it is." She found herself in a position that had her nearly horizontal in fully reclined position. "Except now I can't see out the window," Hattie complained in a whiny tone that made her sound like a child. She slowly moved the seat up into a compromised position where she felt somewhat comfortable but could still see out the side window and windshield as the car went north. She then started adjusting the knobs on the environmental controls.

"How does this work now?"

"Grandma Hattie, you are worse than a toddler. I already had that preset so it's not too hot or too cold."

"Well, right now, Dot, it's too chilly for me."

"Okay, that middle knob there, turn it to the right, until you are in the red. That brings in more heat, though I can't understand why you'd be cold for the life of me here in South Florida."

"Dot, when you get to be 100, you'll realize that furnace inside isn't always on.

Sometimes all that's left is the pilot light."

She merged into traffic on Interstate 95 and headed north. All they saw were cars on either side of them, moving steadily at 80 miles per hour, as she changed lanes and ended up in the center lane of the ten-lane highway.

Hattie then noticed the radio and began pushing the buttons, going from one preset station to the next. "What kind of blasted music you listen to, child?"

"Obviously, the kind you don't like. Use the tuner there to the right and find your own station. I think there's a couple of country stations you can listen to."

Hattie did and fiddled with the knob until she found a country station that had a Conway Twitty song playing. "That's more like it. Hopefully, they'll keep playing these old songs."

"There's an oldies rock station in there somewhere too, Grandma."

"Dot, you know darn good and well, I only listen to country. It describes the human experience better than that old rock music. And what do you kids listening to now? Rap? That's horrible sounding; all loud and using that 'n' word constantly."

"You know about rap?"

"I got me a couple nurses your age who blast that stuff on their I-phone. We all just ignore it and smile at them like we approve. What we are really doing is saying inside, you all just wait until you get to be our ages and am forced to listen to whatever excuse for music, they play fifty or sixty years from now."

Dot laughed. "Oh, Grandma Hattie!

That is funny."

"It wasn't meant to be so, but I suppose it is." Hattie chuckled and then glanced outside her side window. "I surely hate to do this to you, but I got to find me a powder room somewhere."

"Oh Grandma! Okay, just up the highway is a convenience store. I'll get me something to snack on and you can use the restroom. This ain't gonna be an ongoing issue, is it?"

Hattie looked directly at her great granddaughter before replying, "When you get to be my age, with all my plumbing the way it's been modified over the years, you'd be having to go more often too."

Dot took the next available exit where a high sign proclaiming Gull that was seen from miles away showed fuel pump islands and a modern style convenience store. Dot parked her Prius and ran inside to get the snacks and beverages needed, while Hattie remained inside the car, waiting for her great granddaughter to get a clue and come back out to help her. Five minutes later she rushed out and got in.

"God, Grandma did you fart?"

"No honey, I done shit my drawers because you were in an all-fire hurry to get your snacks and left me in here. I would have made it in there simply fine, but it seems your tummy was more important than my bowels.

"My Lord, this new generation gets more and more concerned with their own selves rather than considering others that I've ever seen."

Dot rushed over to her great grandmother's side and opened the door. "I'm so sorry Grandma. I forgot."

"You forgot? I'm the one that mentioned I had to go not more than ten minutes ago. It's lucky for you I got my adult diapers on because I figured something like this was gonna happen."

Dot helped her out, continuously gushing apologies to Hattie while they walked inside the restroom together. It was a tight and narrow place with a sink and a toilet. There was little if any room to move about, let alone change one's adult diaper. Hattie did the hard part, raising her dress high enough for Dot to remove the diaper and found another in Hattie's handbag, along with a package of baby wipes and an added adult sized diaper.

Dot didn't say a word but wondered if this was the curse of getting as old as her great grandmother. "What the heck do they feed you all?"

"Stinks, don't it?"

"Makes me want to gag, Grandma."

"I know child, I know."

"Okay I'm done wiping that up, now what?"

"Just put on the diaper. They're tabs to secure it with. I just thank God we have disposable diapers. Can you imagine putting cloth diaper over this big old butt?"

"This is really queer you know?"

"Honestly, Dot you make this seem unsavory. Just finish up so I can put my dress back down. I may have to stop somewhere and buy me a new slip. This one is ruined."

Dot came up with an idea. "Take off the slip. When we reach North Miami, I'm sure there's a Wal Mart there and you can get you a new one. I got me some scissors to cut off the shoulder straps." She quickly reached inside her purse and pulled out nail scissors, cutting off the straps. The slip fell to the floor where they both saw the brown, soiled ring.

"Just throw it away, Dot." She dropped the dress and smoothed it back in place. She then grabbed her cane when there came a knocking on the door.

"Everything okay in there?" the middle-aged clerk asked through the restroom door. His voice sounded like he smoked a pack of Camels a day. They heard him cough.

"We are done," Hattie announced as she unlocked the door and stepped out. "I would suggest, young man, you get you a scrub brush, bucket of soapy water and a mop to clean this restroom, rather than smoke a cigarette during your next break. It's disgusting in here."

"Yes ma'am," he replied respectfully.

His weathered face took on a red hue of embarrassment.

Dot smiled at him as she went past him and caught up to her great grandmother before exiting the store. "Grandma Hattie, you really gave him a lecture."

"Well, child, it was disgusting in there. Did you see how brown that toilet bowl was? There's no call for that. And that sink, I wouldn't wash a dog's paws in that." Hattie allowed Dot to help her inside the Prius. A moment later they traveled on the freeway, stopping at a Wal Mart in North Miami.

The parking lot appeared full, and they didn't find another space until they were a good two acres away. "Grandma Hattie, next time we do this, I'm gonna register for a handicap sticker and put it on my car here," Dot said pointing at the rearview mirror to allow them the privilege of parking in the disabled parking spaces, though those too were full. "You okay if I go and get you a wheelchair cart?"

"I'll be a fine child. You go ahead and do what you must do to make it right." Hattie watched Dot disappear down the seemingly miles and miles of cars. Five minutes later, she spotted Dot riding a wheelchair cart to the Prius and stopped in front of the car door.

Dot helped her out and into the cart with a basket in front of handlebars. "This might be a fun ride for you Grandma!"

"We'll see child, we'll see." She pressed the reverse switch, backed the mobility aid out to the lane and pressed the switch forward and pressed the accelerator, taking off at a rapid- paced momentum that caused Dot to run after her great grandmother.

"Grandma Hattie, slow down!" Dot yelled after her, but Hattie just smiled and didn't do any such thing until she reached the store's façade. She stopped at the entry where a kindly door greeter in his 70s opened the door for her.

"Welcome to Wal-Mart ma'am." He saw the young twenty-year-old breathlessly catch up to her great grandmother.

"My word child, you got to get yourself in better shape. "You are all breathless and sweaty," Hattie reprimanded Dot. "I asked you to slow down!"

"I bet this here cart is the fastest one here. Is that so, young man?"

"I reckon you are correct, ma'am," the smiling greeter replied. "Is this your caregiver?"

"No, this is my great granddaughter."

"I see," he replied as his smile turned abruptly into a frown.

Both women ignored his shocked expression as they went on inside the vast department store. "You know, Dot this place has nothing on Newberry's or Woolworth. Back in my day, those were the stores to go to, especially in Chicago. I bought this dress at a Woolworth there back in 1958. It doesn't look nearly as sharp on me now as it did then though. Your grandfather and I went shopping there, and they asked if that colored boy was my neighbor's child. I told the cashier there, 'no this is my son.' I got the same reaction that man just gave us."

"Do you regret marrying Gramps?"

"Not a day in my life, child."

"Let's go find you a slip, Grandma Hattie." They moved about the crowded store, meandering around other shoppers until they reached the women's apparel.

Hattie picked out a cellophane package that held a petite woman's slip, a pearl satin fabric. "Wouldn't you rather have a cotton one? This would be hot in this heat and humidity, Grandma Hattie."

She looked up at her great granddaughter, staring at her steadily. "Don't you ever dictate to me what clothes I should or shouldn't wear, young lady."

"I was merely suggesting…"

"Don't even do that!"

"I'm sorry; I won't do it again."

Hattie smiled at her. "That's fine dear. Now let's go to the cashier and get this rung up."

"There's no need, Grandma Hattie, they got those self-service registers now. We only got this one item."

"Self Service? Don't nobody like to talk to each other anymore?"

"We only have this one item, Grandma."

"Lands, this country has changed, and not in a good way neither." They made their way to the banks of cashiers, and most were filled with customers getting their cartloads checked out. She finally wheeled up to an empty self-service kiosk. Dot scanned the package, and Hattie pulled her change purse from the handbag, took note of the charge and handed Dot the ten-dollar bill. "This country's gotten expensive too."

After plucking the receipt from the machine, they placed it inside the plastic Wal-Mart bag.

They came to a security officer and Dot asked the young Black man, "My Grandma need to change into this. Can I show you the receipt as we leave?"

"This is it? Is there anything inside that purse?" He had a big belly that the navy-blue uniform shirt barely concealed his white cotton t-shirt, the buttons strained against his massive belly. Hattie thought they'd pop off his shirt at any moment.

"Young man, I am a great grandmother and have never stolen anything my entire life. You go ahead and check my handbag. But I can assure you, sir I have no intention of ever coming back to this store again." Hattie raised her handbag to him.

His embarrassment appeared clear as he quickly glanced inside. "You all are clear to go inside. Have a wonderful day ma'am." He looked about the store, trying to find an excuse to get away from the old woman.

They ignored his consternation and went inside the restroom, going to the handicap stall. Graffiti written in black permanent markers filled the inside walls. Restroom attendants long ago gave up on removing the offensive, gang-banger literature. Hattie read a certain term that used the 'n' word and the 'f' word quite liberally.

She removed her dress and placed the slip over her body. She gladly covered her thin bony frame. "Long ago, I had an incredibly beautiful body. Now it's a wasted thing; something to store these old bones. I can't even look myself in the mirror no more."

"TMI Grandma," Dot called out from the other side of the door.

"What does that mean?"

"You all are giving me too much information that I really didn't want to hear, Grandma."

"Well, I'm sorry, child." She placed her dress back over her head. "Come in here and zip me up."

"Who zipped you up this morning before I arrived?"

"Miss Agnes the nightshift nurse before she went home at seven this morning."

"You already had your clothes laid out and then you pretend you don't recall going when I showed up! You should be ashamed of yourself Grandma." Dot zipped her dress for her great grandmother.

Hattie laughed at the trick she played on her granddaughter. "I'm sorry honey. I do like to mess with you young ins." She sat back down in the mobile cart and backed herself from the stall. Dot followed behind her stewing in rage.

The parking lot appeared to have filled even more since they arrived. Most cars were twenty to forty years old, had dings and dents on their quarter panels, rust and missing paint on their doors. There weren't just African American and white shoppers anymore as Hattie remembered, but a rainbow coalition of ethnicity going into the massive store. Hattie heard many tongues speak languages other than English, which surprised her. She wondered about that but said nothing as she maneuvered the cart down the parking lot.

Dot helped Hattie from the mobility device and went back into her car. After closing the door, she got behind the wheel and started up the car. She backed out abruptly and sped down the lines of parked cars. She then drove out into traffic without checking first, causing angry blasts from other car horns along with one car's squealing brakes as the driver stepped on the car brakes.

"Dorothy Mae Black, you calm yourself down right now! You hear?" Hattie reacted in frustration.

"You stop treating me and my generation like we are the enemy, and I will."

"Now, you are just being childish."

"How about you Grandma? You just admitted you like poking fun at me by pretending to not remember our trip that you insisted weeks ago we attend. God, you drive me nuts sometimes."

"Don't you go using the Lord's name in vain. That's blasphemous!"

Dot stared straight ahead, ignoring her great grandmother. She drove in silence to the onramp and merged into heavy freeway traffic toward the turnpike at I-95 and Indiantown Road interchange. Most drivers she saw tossed their exact change into the plate and given the green light to continue. Dot was never that good. She slowed to nearly a stop before tossing the five quarters into the tray and getting the green light, nearly causing the driver behind her to brake abruptly, barely avoiding an accident.

In turn it caused an accordion reaction. Somewhere, hundreds of feet down the freeway, someone was distracted and didn't slow down, which caused a collision and several hours of traffic backup.

Neither were aware of the incident behind them. They drove in silence for several miles. Finally, Hattie asked Dot, "In that stall was a lot of graffiti talking about a bunch of nonsense. I don't know why you all seem to like to use that 'n' word so often. Don't you even know what that word means? How foul and evil it is?"

Dot glanced at her for a moment. "What does it mean, Grandma Hattie?"

"Lord have Mercy! That word was a derogatory word. It's what white bigots used to describe a Black man as something inferior and hateful. It was like calling a Jewish man a kike, or a Chinese man a chink.

"Yet, what galls me is how even Black kids use that word against each other. Can you explain that one to me? I hear it all the time from the two custodians and nurses' aides that work there at that nursing home I live in."

"It's called an assisted living facility."

"Oh, fiddle sticks; it's a nursing home, Dot. They put a nice word on a crumby place and expect us old people not to know the difference.

"The only thing that is different is how expensive that place is. All my Social security retirement goes into that place each month.

"But they give me an allowance; an allowance on something I earned for over forty years being a high school history teacher. The nerves of those people.

"Now, answer my question, why in God's name are you kids using that word so casually?"

Dot sighed heavily. "I honestly don't know. I guess the street gangs and such use it and to us, it is just a word that lost its meaning years ago."

"That needs to stop. I saw other things on that wall too. All nonsense of course. Apparently, this girl missed her history classes because she was telling the world how ignorant she was by proclaiming the Holocaust was a hoax orchestrated by the Jews. Henry and your

Great-Great uncle Billy gave their lives because of that 'hoax.' I swear your generation is cursed."

"Was there anything about white power and other non-such?"

"I don't recall, but it wouldn't surprise me."

Dot shook her head. "I'm sorry you had to see that, Grandma Hattie. There's a rest stop a mile up the road. Do you need to relieve yourself?"

"No, but I wouldn't mind stepping out and stretching these old legs a spell." Dot nodded as she went to the exit and took a right. She drove under the trestles overpass and found themselves at a parking lot with a dozen or so other parked cars. Cypress trees, along with shrubs and green grass bordered gravel walking trails that meandered about the Sand Lakes Restoration Area.

"It's close to noon, and my old body is finally warmed up sufficiently. This is a right pretty place, Dot. I smell Spanish moss; must be a pond or swamp nearby." "I reckon that's why this place is called Sand Lakes Restoration Area, grandma."

"Well, where is this Sand Lake?"

"There are markers on the trails that shows how to get there."

"Oh, I see. Well, I ain't gonna walk that trail. I'd break an ankle. It's for young folks. Younger than me anyway. Dot, you go ahead and take me a picture with that fancy cell phone of yours."

Dot smiled at her. "Sure, I can do that, Grandma Hattie." She took off at a run along the trail toward the lake shore. Hattie slowly navigated toward a bench and sat down.

Squirrels and hungry sea gulls flirted about the grass while Hattie looked on. She noticed chickadees, robins and songbirds in the trees overhead.

"You critters are hungry, aren't you? I ain't got nothing to feed you with. I guess Dot bought some stuff for us to snack on later. I'll see if…Oh wait, there is a sign that says I shouldn't be feeding y'all. I guess you all got spoiled by our food and expected handouts all the time. Sorry guys, I can't help you."

Dot came back with a disappointed look upon her tan face wearing a frown of consternation.

"Let's go Grandma. There ain't no lake down there. It's just a swamp with mango trees, Cypress and Sand Oaks. Like you said there are Spanish moss hanging off them trees everywhere."

"Help me up child. I feel much better. I think I got another two hours of driving in me."

"Well, Grandma, it's still four hours before we cross into the Georgia State Line." She did a quick Google search. "Grandma, according to this, we can stop in Jacksonville for the night."

"That's fine child. We can do that then."

Hattie and Dot stopped at a Travel Lodge just outside Jacksonville where the sun seemed to be at its highest point in the early evening. The room they got was the former manager's office. It had a separate bedroom with handicap accessible features for disabled guests. The new office was a separate building out front of the motel with a security lock on the door and a window for the guests to register. Hattie took it all in as Dot used her credit card to finish paying for the room.

Dot walked in first and marveled at its immense size, and with a separate bedroom, felt it was as big as the apartment she lived in. "It's big Grandma."

"It sure is, child. What's this thing on the wall?"

"Grandma, it's a TV set. It's called an HDTV."

"It is a waste for me. I don't watch that stuff no more. I just read or do needlepoint."

"Yes, ma'am," Dot replied half listening to her. "Are you hungry?"

"Yes, I could stand to have a bit of supper before I retire to bed. I am getting powerful sleepy."

"You should have taken a nap." She snapped her fingers as if struck by a thought. "I'll tell you what, I'll drive down to the drive-in up the street and pick up some chicken and grits."

"Child, I don't eat that fried food anymore. Ain't healthy for a body to eat all that disgusting food."

"Ain't so bad," Dot replied in disappointment. "Okay, what would you like?"

"I want a salad with a tuna fish sandwich. If you can get me a juice too, I would be greatly thankful."

"I'll see what I can do, Grandma." She gave Hattie a disappointed look. Hattie sat on the couch in the main room and felt the firmness beneath the cushions and knew a hideaway bed was stored.

"If I was twenty years younger, I'd do Dot a favor and get this bed ready for her. I don't know why she is so smitten with that squawk box. HDTV! It's a waste of good intellect, time and money. If they put that energy and time on inventions to cure cancer, would do better than putting that blasted old thing together."

Dot walked in about that time, catching Hattie by surprise. "I changed my mind, Grandma. I went down to the corner market and grabbed a package of tuna, bread, mayo and relish, along with this salad and packet of dressing. We'll make our supper right here and not go to the expense of fast food, though I was having a hankering for fried chicken. This is about you and this trip I promised you. I can eat chicken anytime I want."

Hattie smiled at her great granddaughter. "My word, child I guess you have done grown up."

Dot also smiled. She finished pulling the food stuff from the paper bag and set it upon the counter near the sink and next to a microwave oven. She searched inside a cupboard and found plates and silverware inside a drawer. She then peeled the wrapping from the package of tuna, opened the jars of mayonnaise and relish, and mixed everything in a microwaveable bowl that was conveniently found inside the microwave.

Hattie watched her work on making their supper with envy. *I really want to help.*

"Can I help you do something Dot?" "You can put mayonnaise on the bread, Grandma. I'll be done here in a jiff."

While Hattie prepared the sandwiches by spreading mayonnaise lightly on each bread slice, Dot asked her, "Grandma can you tell me about Gramps?"

"Lord, child I wondered when you were going to want me to bring all that up. Let me turn on my memory cap." She chuckled and watched Dot roll her eyes.

"Anyway, your great grandfather was a handsome, tall man. You favored him in a lot of ways, your liquid brown eyes, your strong young jaw, reminds me so much of my Henry.

"We married at Uncle William's place in 1936. A year later, your great uncle Henry was born. You never met him because he was killed in Korea in 1952. But that's another story. Your grandfather Charles was born in 1942. Charles married your grandmother in 1970, and your father was born in 1976. He married your mother in 1996, and of course you, the love child no one planned for, come to be in 1995.

"Back to your great grandfather, like I said he was a very strapping young man. I met him years before, but that too is another story. We both graduated from college; I went to Florida State University, and he got his law degree from Northwestern in Chicago. It wasn't easy, but he did get work as a trial lawyer for the public defenders' office eventually.

"Then, those dab-burn Japanese ruined everything when they attacked Pearl Harbor for no good reason." Hattie choked. "If it weren't for that, he would never volunteer to be a pilot. He might still be alive today!"

Dot went over and hugged Hattie as she sobbed. "Grandma, I'm truly sorry I conjured up that awful memory."

Hattie pulled herself from Dot. "It's okay child. When you get to be my age, you have both good and bad memories. You move on is all you can do." She found a tissue and dabbed a tear from her eye.

Dot handed her a plate, and they sat on the couch, eating quietly. Both were thoughtful as they chewed on their salads and sandwiches.

"I surely miss him though," Hattie mused. "I was teaching at Lincoln High School. I taught there until I retired in 1979. That's forty-four years as a history teacher teaching living history. I think I taught in the most valuable time of our lives.

"The day I got the news, an officer and chaplain showed up. I was teaching about the emancipation proclamation.

Another teacher, Mr. Barnes took over and we went to the teachers' lounge where they informed me, he was shot down over Italy and killed. I never bothered to marry again. I dated plenty of men, but the moment they saw my three boys, they made excuses for not ever coming back again."

"What about others, like us?"

Hattie seemed lost in thought. "I guess I was looking for all the wrong men for all the right reasons."

"So, dating a man of color was out of the question?" Dot asked in astonishment.

"I'm sorry honey but no man could hold a candle to my Henry, regardless of what skin color they had. Henry was one in a million. I had plenty of male companions who I dated on occasion. They were just friends; fellow teachers who I talked politics with on occasion."

Hattie chuckled. "Oh, there was one time I'll never forget. Your grandfather was seven or eight, I think. My friend, a nice young gentleman named Roger Schwartz came to my door for a coffee. I had just gotten Charlie to bed when the doorbell chimed.

"He jumped out of bed wearing his night shirt and nothing else and answered the door. Well, that nightshirt was Henry's old T-shirt, and it was too big for Charlie. So, when he answered the door with me running behind him, his personal affairs were all that poor man saw. The shirt fell off that little boy's body before he opened the door." Hattie laughed.

"Oh my God!" Dot exclaimed in shock.

"How embarrassing for you both."

"Come Charlie's next birthday he got a present from Roger. It was pajamas with elastic on the pants to hold them up."

"I take it from the name that he was white."

"Naturally; like I said, I couldn't seriously consider anyone after Henry."

Dot stared at Hattie with a sense of anger in her voice when she spoke her mind. "Frankly, Grandma, I think you was being hypocritical."

"How can you say such a thing, child?" The comment hurt Hattie to the core.

"Think about it, Grandma. You fall for Great Grandfather Black. Why? Well, you haven't told me why yet. You keep saying you'll get to it when we visit the museum. But then you say after he was killed, that you couldn't bring yourself to go after another man of color. That, to me, is hypocritical."

Hattie sat there watching her great granddaughter. She didn't have words to express her feelings at that time. Tears welled up and slowly cascaded down her weathered cheeks. "All I can say child, is that I'm sorry if you believe what my love for my one man meant I was being hypocritical toward other Black men. I never meant anything of the sort. I never considered myself racist, but the opposite. I feel powerful tired now."

They finished, Dot gathered the plates and washed them. Hattie yawned and gently pulled herself up. "I'm going to bed."

"Good night, Grandma."

Hattie awoke the next morning, around 4:30. Dot was still asleep. She walked slowly about using her cane to guide her into the darkened kitchen area, bumping into the table and counter. The commotion caused Dot to stir. "Go back to sleep child. I just want to brew me some coffee."

"I'll get it for you Grandma. They got this new thing called Keurig. It makes individual coffee."

"I never heard of such a thing. Okay child, make me some coffee then."

Dot got out of bed wearing a shift with thin spaghetti straps and gauze-like cotton fabric. She began the process of turning on the coffee maker, pulling out the individual pod of coffee and placing it into a chamber, placing a ceramic mug underneath and pulling down the top, which punched a hole into the pod and began pouring coffee into the mug. One of the straps from her shift kept falling off her copper-colored shoulder and she kept sliding it back over.

"I'll be," Hattie expressed in awe. "But I wanted to make an entire pot, darling." "Grandma, people don't have time to waste on a pot of coffee no more. They barely have time to run off to work and make it on time."

"You know, child there's a simple solution to this; get up earlier."

"But then we wouldn't get enough sleep.

Today, we must take our work home with us…"

"So, did I Dot. All those years as a teacher, I didn't leave my work there at the school. I had to bring it home. I had over two hundred quizzes, tests, essays and final reports to read and grade. I still made me a full pot of coffee after getting a good seven hours sleep. I didn't bother with that thing over there either. That's what I didn't have time for," Hattie pointed in the direction of the TV set mounted on the wall.

Dot didn't have an argument as the coffee maker ended its cycle and she pulled the cup out, handing it to Hattie. "I suppose I should get showered and dressed. We still got a way to go yet."

Hattie nodded before taking a sip and smiled with gratification. "At least this thing makes a good cup of coffee."

She watched Dot run into the bathroom. A moment later Hattie heard the shower nozzle spray water into the tub. She saw the bathroom earlier this morning when she had to relieve herself. It wasn't disabled-friendly.

It did have grab bars, but she didn't have anything to sit on. She made up her mind right then to bathe in the bathroom sink before dressing and going out the door.

Hattie watched Dot leave the bathroom holding her shift over her body, protectively as she grabbed her change of clothes from her overnight bag and ran back into the bathroom. A moment later she came out dressed and smiled radiantly with bright white teeth. The bathroom light behind her cast an angelic beam of light off her. "You gonna get ready?"

"Yes, child, yes, but I ain't about to get in that tub with nothing to sit on. I'll just take me a bird bath over the sink in there."

"They should have one somewhere in there, Grandma Hattie."

"I didn't see one by the tub last night, unless they got it stowed somewhere."

"That's probably what it is. Dang, the office ain't open yet."

"Oh, don't worry yourself about it child. I take bird baths all the time. I don't want no man to come and bathe me. It ain't proper."

"There isn't a female nurse for when you want to take a bath?"

"Sometimes there is, sometimes there ain't. It just depends on the time of day. But at least, no one forces the issue. I told them, Henry was the only man in my life, besides my pa of course and personal doctor, who ever had a right to see me naked. The day I die, then I suppose the mortician will have that right too."

"Good for you Grandma Hattie."

Hattie took her cane and cup of coffee with her and went into the bathroom. She left the door open as she slowly undressed herself. While she did so she used a washcloth to soap up her flesh and used a damp towel to rinse herself off. Finally, she used a bath towel to dry herself.

Unlike her great granddaughter, there was no modesty. She walked out naked and asked Dot, "I know it's a lot to ask, child, but could you put on my adult diaper for me? It's them dang old tabs that get me.

It's okay, I already cleaned myself. There ain't nothing dirty."

"Well, Grandma, that's not a problem. I'll do it. I guess you gave me a right to see you naked too."

"You are kin, child. There ain't nothing wrong with your own kin seeing you like this. But a stranger? Forget it."

Dot shrugged but went ahead and placed Hattie's diaper on. "Okay, I'm done. Here's your brassiere and slip. You got another dress?"

"Yes, in that bag, I have one all nice and folded. It's the one I got when that cashier mistook your grandpa for a neighbor boy. 'Oh, what a nice colored boy!' This is what she said upon seeing him with me. 'Are you babysitting him?' No, I said. He's mine. The look she gave me was priceless, yet it conjured a passion deep inside, same as my pa."

"What do you mean by passion Grandma?"

"Passion is an emotion. Hand me my cross first." Dot placed the cross necklace behind her neck and fastened it. Her hair was pinned up.

"Thank you. As I was telling you, passion is an emotion and a state of mind. It can be love, hate, anger, you name it. In the case of that woman and Pa, hate, pure and low-down evil, passionate hate."

"I guess I've been pretty much insulated from that because I never noticed it."

"Child, you are naïve. There's nothing wrong with that. Your parents raised you to not take notice of how people see you. Times have changed too. Most times, just as Martin Luther King had hoped, people now-a-days are judged by their character, not by their skin color.

"Sometimes, at least as I see it, a racist will crawl out of the woodwork, like that Walmart greeter yesterday. Yes, I supposed he could justify his reaction in some manner, but it doesn't change the truth that he is a true-blue racist."

"Was Great-great grandpa White the first racist you ever come across?"

"Yes, child he was. He had his good points, but his undying passion was his hatred to all people not white, Christian and a Democrat, as many were back then.

"That last part all changed thanks to Eleanor Roosevelt. She was progressive. Her uncle was Theodore Roosevelt, and she was a lot like him in many ways, including his feelings that all people are created equal. A man's skin tone shouldn't have nothing to do with his inalienable rights."

"I know that from the history books I read."

"Yes, Dot, but I lived it." She combed her hair and brushed her teeth. She drank down the last of her coffee and said, "I'll tell you more later when we get there."

Dot helped her out the entry and into the parking lot. She helped her great grandmother into the Prius and closed the door when two police cruisers rolled into the parking lot.

Two Jacksonville Police officers raced out from their cars and pounded on a motel room door above them. The door barely opened, and the first officer barged inside, followed by t h e second.

Dot stood frozen in place as she saw the officers drag a young Black man down the stairs. His hands were cuffed, yet the two white officers appeared pleased at punching him in his sides and face with their black leather gloved fists.

They then tasered him and caused him to lose consciousness before they threw him in the back of a Chevrolet Impala. A woman ran down the stairs screaming, "He didn't do anything!"

"He must have done something," one of the officers replied. "Look at him; how black he is. He's got to be a criminal. We're taking him in for questioning anyway.

We'll get a confession from him."

Both Dot and the other woman looked at the officer who said that with a bemused expression of shock and disbelief. "Well, what are you arresting him for?" Dot asked, though she didn't get the answer she expected.

"You mind your own damn business, girl, or you can go into custody too," the second young police officer replied, his face red with anger.

"If you want to know," the first officer answered, "We are arresting him on suspicion of an armed robbery last night at the market just up the street from here.

"Now, get the hell out of our business and drive away to wherever y'all are going!" He got into his cruiser and drove out of the motel parking lot, followed by his partner. The woman, whose skin appeared a shade darker than Dot's sat on a stair and cried.

Dot shook with passion at the officers. She got inside the car and fiddled with the keys, though the ignition was a start button. Hattie watched her with a look of concern on her wrinkled face. "What is wrong with this country?" Dot asked herself aloud.

"Ain't nothing wrong with the country child. This country has always been this way. The people here are the ones with something wrong with them."

"I don't understand." Her fingers shook violently. Hattie reached over and touched them, caressed her trembling fingers with her cold digits, and stroked them tenderly, trying to get Dot to calm down.

Dot spoke through clinched teeth, her jaw tight with anger, "He didn't do anything wrong. He was in that store ahead of me. He bought a pack of cigarettes and a bottle of beer. You know, one of them big twenty-four-ounce things and left.

"Then I bought our supper. I just don't understand it." Dot started crying as tears rolled down her face. "I should have told them I did it. What would they had done then?"

"You'd make them look foolish and truly racist." She moved her arm over her trembling body and hugged her. "It's okay child. You're learning the truth about passion, hate and intolerance. There ain't a thing wrong with that."

Dot finally recovered. "I'm going to that police precinct where they took him and tell them they arrested the wrong man. He wasn't the one.

"There was another that followed me. He was Black but had a spiderweb tattoo on his right cheek and mess of other tattoos on his neck and arms."

She then noticed the keys for the first time and laughed. "A lot of good these would have done. This car has a push button; no call for keys. You must think I've lost my mind; turning as senile as you."

She started the car and backed it up. Hattie buckled herself in and watched Dot drive, using her cellphone to navigate her to the precinct station. "I'm sorry Grandma, I didn't mean you were senile.

"I know. Your anger and frustration have gotten the best of you. I know you meant nothing by what you said. It ain't no big deal."

She saw Dot stop the car in front of a brick-and-mortar building. A sign outside proclaimed it to be the Twelfth Precinct of Jacksonville Police. "Honey, you'll need to help me out of this car, so I can be there to help keep you calm."

Dot glanced at her, realized what she said and nodded. "You know I would say something I'd regret later."

"Yes, child. I don't want to be catching me a Greyhound to Montgomery, while you languished in a jail cell waiting for a judge to hear your side of what might happen if I stayed put in this here Japanese car." Dot helped her out. She then went directly inside with Hattie following her.

Hattie caught up to her as she stood below a raised dais where the police sergeant sat and listened with patience to Dot's recollection of what happened last night.

"Now sir, I don't know that man you all arrested from Adam. I'm just a witness. But I swear, you got the wrong man," Dot argued.

"That man that was arrested, has a rap sheet as long as my arm, ma'am."

"Maybe he does, I don't know anything about that, sir. But what I do know is last night and he did not rob that store. I did see another man follow me in though. He had a mess of tattoos on his arms, neck and one of a spider web on his right cheek right here," Dot showed him.

The sergeant then gave her a double take. "Are you certain about the tattoo, I mean?"

"As certain as you are sitting there," Dot replied with a sober expression on her face.

He got up from his perch and left the area a moment. He returned with one of the arresting officers. He gave her a sour grape look. The sergeant announced, "It appears you grabbed the wrong one. This witness here claims it was more than likely Lincoln Barnes who done it, not Brittle, as you suspected."

"Are you sure?" The officer asked her with doubt etched in his voice.

"Yes, sir." Dot gave him the same determined look as when the sergeant asked.

"Okay, I guess I'll release him then." He left them and the sergeant resumed sitting in his cat bird seat, looking down at her and Hattie.

"Let's go to Montgomery child," Hattie beamed at Dot, happy and proud of her great granddaughter.

Hattie watched the scenery whizzed by at over 80 miles per hour in the early morning as the sun rose behind them on I-10. Traffic was light but steady. Structured suburbs gave way to more rural farmland and individual farmhouses, centuries old.

Interstate 10 flowed into Interstate 75, and they went north into Georgia. The scenery changed into more rolling hills and small tenant farms cropped up where poor Black and white people broke their backs trying to earn enough to keep from losing their land every year. Dot got off the freeway at the Cordele exit and drove northwest on Highway 280. It took them through Americus and Plains. Hattie smelled the heady aroma of tobacco filling the car's cabin. It was a light floral scent.

"I dearly miss that smell, Dot." "What smell is that?"

"Tobacco flowers, honey.

Unfortunately, it doesn't smell nothing like that when they grind the leaves into cigarettes."

"I heard, they add rat poison to it to keep people addicted," Dot said

"If they did, it was long after my pa passed. That was one thing he didn't do; add rat poison to the tobacco he grew.

"This country has gone to ruin if that is the case. Poisoning our own people like that. Those growers should burn in hell for that!"

"Once we reach Columbus, Georgia, we'll go directly west into Alabama and Montgomery."

"I was but a child, but we went to Columbus once. I think it was the county fair that we went to. Pa almost got himself into a fight with a judge because he picked this Black man's tobacco leaf over his and won first place prize."

"How could Great-great Grandpa live that way? Always hating and never accepting," Dot inquired aloud to herself.

"Child, if I had an answer to that, I'd win me a Nobel prize. As I said before, Hate is a passion. It eventually eats you up from the inside, like cancer. He didn't go to my wedding, but I did attend his funeral in 1961. Uncle William was still alive, and he provided the casket that we agreed on."

"Casket?"

"I'll tell you more when we get there," Hattie said with finality in her voice.

"Yes, ma'am; oh, look there's someone broke down on the highway." They approached a pair of young men next to a pick-up truck with its hood up. Their coffee-toned skin shined in the mid-day sun as they wiped the sweat from their brows.

A Georgia State trooper was also pulled over directing traffic along as they apparently awaited a tow truck to take them into the next town.

"Should we offer them a ride, Grandma?"

"No child, it looks like that trooper has everything handled."

"Police aren't always the bad guys, are they Grandma?"

"Child, police are human too. They err at times. You proved that earlier. I'd say most police are decent and hard-working. I recall back in Chicago in '68 when those riots occurred outside the Democratic Convention. I saw a lot of police helping people get around that melee. I'd say those police officers were helping the decent folks, white or black, to steer clear.

"All those hippies, Yippies and Black Panthers, were the troublemakers. They were the ones who won the Presidency for Richard Nixon. As sure as I'm sitting here in this Japanese car, Nixon would not have won. He wasn't popular. I thought he was an ugly man with that long and pointy nose of his."

Dot laughed. "Oh, here's the Columbus skyline, Grandma. It sure is a pretty city from back here."

"They're all pretty from back here, Dot. It's when you are inside that you get to see the passion and the hate. It's when you go inside is when it turns ugly."

Dot nodded as they continued west. They stopped briefly at nearby Golden Ball Park. They noticed all the Army trucks and Humvees rolling past them along with the overhead exit signs announcing Fort Benning and the town of Benning. "This place is huge Grandma!"

"You never been in a military base before?"

"No ma'am," Dot replied, her eyes big as saucers at all the military vehicle traffic that surrounded them.

"It ain't no different than when I first visited my Henry outside Tuskegee. That entire little college town was transformed overnight, it seemed. It didn't occur to me how much trouble I caused when I showed up though. There was no tolerance when it came to us. We were pariahs in their eyes when they saw him with me."

"It's different now though, right Grandma?"

"I suppose, but don't be all-fired certain on that account. There are still some very narrow-minded people running around."

They crossed the Alabama border an hour later and traffic was steady. Lines of cars moved on the highway divided and flowing at a good clip of over 70 miles per hour until they reached Interstate 85, which took them south and west to Montgomery.

"It looks like we had an enjoyable time Grandma. You want to get something to eat first?"

Hattie looked exhausted as she turned her head to her great-granddaughter. "Child, can we do this tomorrow morning? I am powerful tired."

"I'll find us a motel then."

"That's fine child, that's fine."

Dot spotted a Motel Six and they parked the Prius. Dot walked into the office first and got their room before returning and getting inside, driving in front of the room. "I have to warn you; it may not be as nice as the one in Jacksonville."

Hattie nodded as she opened the door and allowed Dot to help her out the car door. When the door opened before them, it was as Dot suspected, a standard room with twin queen beds aligned next to each other and a nightstand with lamp that sat on top between the two beds. Hattie got on the bed, laid down and fell right to sleep.

After midnight, Hattie awoke. She felt disoriented, as if fog or veil covered her body. The TV set was on, but the volume was muted. It took a moment to realize Dot wore earbuds and she heard everything being said between the two actors. "What time is it, Dot?"

She didn't respond. She saw Hattie try to get out of bed and the movement caught her attention. "Grandma, you are still alive!"

"Well, sure I'm still alive. What a silly thing to say. I've waited 90 years for this day to finally arrive. What time is it child?"

Dot looked at the digital clock on the DVD player. "12:02," she replied attempting to plug the buds back inside her ears.

Hattie sat on the edge of the bed for a few minutes still trying to get her bearings. She felt as befuddled as a drunken sailor. "Tarnation, I feel out of sorts right now." She stared at Dot.

"What was that grandma?"

"You might as well undo those things from that there TV so I can watch the movie too. It's *Steel Magnolias*, ain't it?"

Dot nodded while she removed the earphone cord from the TV and the volume came loud and rich as Sally Field's character talked to Julia Roberts Character. "How'd you know?"

"I watched all those kinds of movies related to the south, child."

"How was it like? Living in the south back then, I mean."

"It was no different than living anywhere else I suppose. Except for Pa, it was all right.

You see Dot, Pa and I didn't agree completely. His passion toward the Black folk was the biggest factor. One day he found me writing a letter to my pen pal. Uncle William spilled the beans and let out who the pen pal was.

'You ain't writing no letter to that colored boy. I forbid it.'

'I'll do as I please, Pa. You ain't got no call for telling me what to do,' "I told him. He then tried to strike me across my face. He hit me so hard, I was knocked to the ground. I saw blood pouring from my mouth. He then dragged me outside, over by a willow tree.

"With his free hand he broke off a willow limb, raised my dress, pulled down my drawers and tried to whip my fourteen-year-old behind.

"I ran into our house bawling and carrying on. I was angrier at Pa than hurt by what he ordered I do. I didn't even bother to pull my knickers back up. They were still wrapped around my ankles.

"It wasn't much of a house, mind you. Billy and I shared a bed in the same room as the family gathering area, the kitchen and the wood burning stove. Ma and Pa shared the bedroom. There was no privacy and more than anything, I wanted desperately to be left alone."

I remembered Billy trying to comfort me, but I didn't want any of it.

'Go and leave me alone!' "I told him. I was so mad and humiliated; I didn't notice what he was staring at until he went outside. I then noticed my raised dress. I was madder still because he didn't say anything; just stared at my private parts.

"So, what happened Grandma Hattie?"

"What else? That night while everyone was asleep, I left and never looked back. The only regret I had was not being invited to Billy's funeral in 1944. He died fighting the Japs on Iwo Jima.

Ma wrote to me, telling me what happened, how the funeral was and all. "Billy and I did more than share a bed in that rundown tenant shack. We shared secrets. He knew who Henry was and never told Pa anything. I knew about Billy too.

"Dot, he admitted he preferred men over women, or boys over girls, though Billy knew it was a sin, and he would surely go to hell for it.

"He knew I left that night after Pa beat me, but didn't tell our parents. I never told anyone but you about your great-great uncle.

"It wasn't until a few days after I got to Uncle William's place, did I write to Ma telling her where I was. She wrote back and figured she knew and thought it was for the best. At least, she wrote, you are with decent, Christian kinfolk.

"That's not saying Pa's kinfolk weren't bad. They were basically good; except they had the same hatred that Pa had. They proudly raised the stars and bars every morning, donned their white robes at night and burned crosses. They lived north of Macon. Uncle William lived in the town of Celebration in Florida. I'll explain more about Uncle William in the morning when we go and visit that museum.

"Florida, though it's south, ain't got the same southern attitude. Well, I take that back; they don't show that same attitude in the same manner. Everything was still segregated.

"I found that to be true even in Chicago. Henry and I weren't allowed in some restaurants and nightclubs. I don't know what it was about a man's skin color that caused such anxiety among some white people. It's a pigment for goodness sakes. It wasn't until after Martin Luther King that things finally changed; officially that is."

Dot stared at her great grandmother a long time before she could reply. "I never imagined. I'm surprised there are any African Americans still around."

"Trust me, it wasn't from lack of trying. By 1925 the Ku Klux Klan had over two million members. They made it into a social organization like the Rotary Club or the Elks. But their hate, their intimidation and their ideology were the same."

"It all makes no sense. Why are there so many people? Are there that many bigots in this country?"

"The short answer, honey is yes. How many people you think live here now?"

"I suppose there be over 300 million."

"Okay, now just suppose that one percent of the total population has nothing but hate to motivate their day to day lives. Well, you do the math college girl."

She laid the remote on the bed in an act of shocked amazement. "I never considered we had so many people like that. But I would imagine these people were like Great-great Grandpa White, poor and ignorant."

"Dot, I've met racists with PhD's, business leaders with million-dollar bank accounts who wouldn't give a hoot toward a person of color. Then there are those, like us who may not believe they be racists but might say or do something that might be construed as insulting to someone.

"I know I've been accused of that by my former students. I even had a close friend and fellow teacher accuse me of going after my Henry because of the guilt that occurred with his father. That what I was doing was racist in its intent."

"Is it Grandma?"

"I guess after we are done with the visit to that museum later this morning, you can make up your own mind. What I say now won't mean a hill of beans, child.

Not meaning to change the subject, but you should try to get some sleep, Dot. I aim to get an early start when the rooster crows."

"Grandma you always get an early start. Don't you ever sleep in?"

"Never had and never will; why I think God made us take naps in the afternoon. It does a body wonders. Now turn that blasted thing off. I never did like the end of that movie anyway. Shelby should never had died."

Dot did as she was told. A blanket of darkness filled the room. Hattie barely saw Dot's darkened figure move about slowly. She removed her clothes, pulling back the covers and getting in her bed. "Goodnight, Grandma."

"Goodnight, child." Hattie watched the dark ceiling after she laid back down, still clothed in the floral dress she bought at a Woolworth in 1958 with Dot's grandfather. She had already requested in her will that she wanted that dress worn for her final viewing. *It will be pleasant to see the cashier and me wearing this dress. I'm ready Henry, but I want to get through this one last thing first.*

Hattie closed her eyes and saw his soft brown eyes appear in her dreams, as they always did. She loved seeing him in her dreams. *I wish you hadn't gone when you did; how you did. You sacrificed so the rest of us could correct the wrongs from the past. Henry, you'd be proud of this country now. Unfortunately, the passion, the hate is still here. I can't explain why. I suppose some people are just born to hate.* She fell asleep on that thought.

SPIKE & RUFUS

Spike's real name was Silas Lee Black, but his crew always nicknamed him Spike for the film director. He was a big and tall man in his thirties. He had a smattering of tattoos from earlier stints in other county jails in Georgia. He awoke first outside a field of green leafy crops lined in long rolls as far as his eyes could see.

Rufus, a dopey looking man with baldhead and indentation on the side of his skull from when someone threw a cue ball at his head, was always Rufus. He too was a big man with dark chocolate complexion. His mother didn't know who his father was and just named him that because she thought the name fit in a Macon, Georgia ghetto. She was fifteen when she had him.

Rufus remembered giving Spike a high-fives as they left that Walmart and hightailed it from the parking lot with half a dozen employees running after them. He figured they had carried out their planned escape. He drove Spike for two hours, then he took a turn off the highway, went down a rural road for a quarter of a mile before pulling up to an abandoned tobacco farm and spent the rest of the early morning sleeping.

At noon, he awoke to the sound of a tractor rolling past them. "Where is we headin' cuzz?" Rufus asked Spike as he stretched and yawned from the back bed of the Dodge truck.

Spike rubbed the growth on his chin. His mouth tasted bitter and felt dry. "I need some attitude adjustment first, Rufus. Then, I suppose we go into

Columbus for a spell. We need to ditch this truck, though."

"This here is a farm, ain't it?"

"I reckon."

"Let's borrow one of their trucks?" "I suppose we could." Spike looked around and saw nothing but rows of tobacco plants with their broad leaves. "You got some more of that attitude adjustment, Rufus?"

Rufus smiled as he pulled from his satchel a small plastic bag of white powder. It was Chrystal meth, crushed into a fine powder.

"We can't smoke that no more, Rufus!"

"It's cool cuzz. I got me a straw and we can snort it like coke."

"That's gonna burn dude." He sat inside the truck thinking of options as Rufus pulled out the straw and made a line of meth. He snorted it quickly through the straw and choked and then sneezed.

"God damn that is wicked. Burns like hell too."

"You got a needle?"

"No, I don't shoot that shit up. I heard it could kill you."

Finally, Spike couldn't stand it any longer. He took the straw from Rufus, who drew a line along the truck's hood. Spike took a deep breath, snorted out a wad of snot from his left and right nostril, then sucked up the drug through the straw. It burned like no other drug ever could. But the euphoria; the high came and he smiled as his demon inside went back to sleep. "I can function now." He handed the straw back to Rufus. "Let's go borrow a farmer's truck."

They grabbed their stuff and walked a couple of miles down the dirt road when they came upon a pair of dogs who barked at them. Neither dog appeared that intimidating or big, and they cowered behind a tractor and hay baler. The two escaped convicts walked with cautious regard when a tall and lean man in his sixties showed up from a barn, wiping his greasy hands on an oily rag. "Can I help you with something, boys?"

"Yes, sir," Spike spoke up, pulling the baseball cap off his head, showing his kinky black hair all disheveled and dirty looking. "Our truck broke down back there a mile or so up the road. We were wondering if you could tow us to the nearest mechanics' shop. We be grateful, sir."

"I see," the farmer replied. "I'm handy with fixing vehicles myself. I can go down there and see if I can help you out."

"You don't have to do that sir," Rufus piped up, suspecting their secret would be revealed the moment he spotted Sumpter County Jail on the side of the truck they stole.

"Oh, I don't mind. What farmer you all work for?"

"Oh, we just got hired on this morning from a job agency."

"A job agency? I've never heard of such a thing. Probably that Carter fella. He does a lot of peculiar stuff in these parts."

"Yeah, that's the guy who hired us; Carter," Spike told him.

"Okay then. I'll go grab my keys and we'll head over there." They watched him disappear inside the barn and Rufus pulled Spike aside.

"This can't continue cuzz."

"I know that nigger," Spike replied in a harsh whisper. "Now, as soon as we get there, you take care of him, and we borrow his truck."

"Why me?"

"Because you've done this sort of thing before. You be the one with aggravated assault on your rap sheet. Mine only has burglary and grand theft."

Rufus looked at him uncertainly. "Most of that was because they pissed me off. He ain't done that to me. Just the opposite, Spike. He been nothing but nice and respectable."

"You don't have to beat him up. Just knock him out for a spell."

"You boys ready?" The tall and lean farmer stuck a toothpick in his mouth as he headed in the direction of a vintage 60s GMC with toolbox sitting in the back. "One of you will have to sit in the back unless you want to straddle that gear shift between your legs. Second gear gets a bit hairy, if you get my drift." He smiled at the thought.

"I'll sit in the back," Rufus volunteered.

Spike went to the passenger side and got in. A loud metallic grinding noise occurred when he slammed the door shut. The farmer then got inside and closed the door. He had a holstered .38 attached to the belt of his trousers.

"I took the liberty to call Carter, but he must've been out in the field. Cell phone reception around here ain't the best. I left a message that I got his truck fixed and will be expecting you soon."

Spike swallowed hard as his mahogany skin took on a paler hue than a second ago.

"Thank you, sir I truly appreciate it."

He smiled at him as he engaged the clutch and started the truck. He then moved the gear shift in reverse and checked both mirrors, back out from in front of the barn. Once he was out on the road, he turned abruptly right and shifted into first gear and moved forward. "Let's get you fixed up and on the road again." Spike watched the hayfield pass by then the tobacco field came into view. The truck came up suddenly and they passed that.

"That be it sir," Spike announced.

The farmer skidded to a stop. "You should have given me better warning young man. I don't recall Carter having a Dodge. I recall he swore by Ford. I always ribbed him on his choices of vehicles."

He shifted the truck in reverse and backed up forty feet to the truck. "Open the hood, so I can take a look."

The old farmer walked slowly from the driver's seat to the back of the truck. The toolbox was already open. "I see you opened the box for me. I appreciate that. Help me up so I can pull my tools down and see if I can fix whatever's wrong with it."

Rufus, who stood behind the farmer, smiled when he swung the rubber mallet against his skull. The farmer took an intake of breath, but fell to the ground, unconscious. Rufus then pulled the handgun from the holster and placed it behind his back. "Don't just stand there, idiot, let's go."

"I didn't see you do nothing," Spike replied. He stood flatfooted over the farmer's prostrate form. He bent down and felt his pulse on the jugular of his neck.

"He ain't dead."

"You told me not to kill him. I found that rubber mallet laying in that toolbox and figured it was the least lethal method. Everything else was metal-like and if I swung that upside his head, it could have been deadly. Now let's go."

Spike got up and ran to the passenger side and slammed the door. "We still going to Columbus first?"

"Yeah, that be okay." Rufus shifted into first and sped away, rapidly shifting gears and leaving the county truck and unconscious farmer behind. They eventually found themselves back on the main highway, a road sign showing Columbus was twenty-five miles away. Right away, Rufus could tell the truck was not geared for highway driving. It constantly veered sharply to the right. There wasn't any power steering on this fifty-five-year-old pickup. "Damn, man, this is shit to drive."

"So long as it gets us to Columbus. We can ditch this ride and take the city bus." He saw how hard Rufus fought to keep control. The truck also seemed to belch and sputter over fifty miles per hour. Twice the truck stopped running altogether. Rufus had to move off the highway and restart the old GMC. Then, it went maybe ten miles down the highway before it died a third and final time. "You know anything about fixing this damn thing?"

Spike's eyes got big when he simply replied, "No."

"Then we're in big trouble. This thing ain't going nowhere." He got out of the truck and opened the hood, pushing it up. Smoke and steam came up from the grease covered engine. It smelled of old oil. Rufus couldn't do more than look dumbly inside the engine compartment, as if something would magically pop up telling him what the problem was. He walked back inside the cab and closed the door.

He looked in his rearview mirror and paled when he spotted a Georgia State trooper pull off the highway and slowly moved up behind them to a stop. "Shit, nigger! State Patrol done come and stop behind us."

Spike saw him too. A big Black trooper wearing a robin's egg blue shirt and opened collar. He pulled his Smokey Bear hat out and placed it on his head.

He slowly walked to the passenger side of the truck. "Well, hello sir. Our truck has broken down," Spike greeted the trooper in a rapid-fire story.

"You all got license and registration for this vehicle?"

"I must be honest with you sir, we ain't got none of that here," Rufus replied. "We borrowed the truck from my cousin down near Americus."

"I see. You all want to step out of the truck please. I'll need to call this in." Both men hesitantly pulled themselves from the broke down pickup and ended up between the old GMC and the trooper's Dodge Charger. They heard him calling in to dispatch. Both had been around the wrong side of the law long enough to know what was being said between the radio-speak.

Spike wanted to run so badly. He knew the gig was up. He noticed a Toyota Prius drive pass him and an elderly woman, as ancient looking as sin itself, watching the scene play by. She was a stranger, yet he felt some sort of connection to her; like a Deja vu moment.

Rufus stood stone still, like a statue. He stood at a position of parade-rest. It was a habit from years as a prisoner or convict. But also, he purposely did that to conceal the farmer's handgun until the right moment arrived.

The trooper stepped out and motioned the young men to the side of the road. "I'm gonna need your names and addresses please. I should have asked for that first but, I guess my mind was on other things."

"Well, sir I'm Silas Lee Black," Spike replied. "I am currently between residences, Trooper Murdock?"

"What was your last known address?"

"Go to hell, nigger," Rufus yelled as he pointed the handgun against the trooper's head and shot him directly. It happened so fast; both fell back in surprise. The trooper's face showed nothing but a peaceful solitude as his body fell to the ground. As it happened, Rufus' timing couldn't have been better; all four lanes of traffic were void of cars coming or going.

"Quick, let's drag him next to the truck."

Spike could only do what he was told and didn't—couldn't—think. For the first time in his short life, he saw a murder. He helped Rufus drag the dead trooper next to the truck.

Rufus then traded the uniform shirt for the stolen Bud-Lite t-shirt. It was a perfect fit. He then placed the Smokey Bear hat over his bald head.

"You gonna have to sit in the back seat, like you were my prisoner," Rufus told Spike. "You said while we were on work detail, you got kin down in Florida?"

Spike didn't have the words. He just nodded dumbly. He watched Rufus pull the trooper's utility belt with holster and Glock 13, the nine-millimeter official sidearm, and secured it around his waist. "We are gonna fry now, aren't we? We done killed a trooper; A Georgia State Trooper, Rufus. What?"

"You just stay cool man. It's all gonna work out. We are going to spend time in Florida with your kinfolk. Then one night we just sneak out, head to Tampa and get the hell out of this country. I know where Celebration is. I found it on the Google map app on my smartphone."

"Oh God have mercy!"

"Let me put these cuffs on you." Spike turned around and allowed his partner to place the cuffs loosely around his wrists and secure them. They then went together to the Charger. Rufus placed Spike in the back seat, and he got inside the driver's seat.

Rufus sat inside the patrol car searching for anything that would reveal this unit's number, when dispatched called in, "Unit 64, 10-38?" He grabbed the mic from the Motorola and hesitated before he called back.

"Unit, 64, 10-22. I was able to help the driver. I am 10-8 now."

"Copy Unit 64, 14:45."

"What you gonna do now?" Spike asked in a state of awe at Rufus' ability.

"We drive to the Florida-Georgia line and ditch this car. Then we hitchhike to Celebration where we lay low with your kinfolk." Rufus checked for a clearing and pulled out, taking a right on the US 27 highway entrance and headed south. A sign showed Tallahassee as 481 miles away. "I hope we can get away with this. My great-great grand pappy was lynched for less than what we done. His name was Artemus, and my grandfather told us he was the biggest, baddest chicken thief in Polk County. The story is, he went to this chicken farm and stole a dozen hens. The farmer caught him, and he was lynched.

"This is ten times worse, Rufus. If we get caught, it be a lethal injection. I heard about that shit. Ain't no fun at all; getting poisoned. I'd much rather be hung than have poison injected into my arm."

"You a stupid nigger! What do you think you inject yourself every time you get high? It sure as hell ain't good for you. It's poison as sure as you are sitting back there! You just ain't done no lethal dose yet.

I assure you though, your day will come." "How much longer do I need to be cuffed up like this. It's uncomfortable." "When we get to the state line, I'll release you, but not before."

"You about the biggest asshole I ever run across, Rufus."

"Just play the part. We got us a long drive ahead of us."

"This better be worth the trouble, Rufus.

I don't want no poison shot up my arm."

THE DRUG HOUSE

While Rufus drove the Charger with one hand on the wheel, his right hand stroking the barrel of the pump action shotgun absent mindedly that was secured to a gunrack, Spike napped but suddenly awoke. "Rufus, I smell Meth cooking."

"What do you mean, Cuz? I don't smell nothing."

"You can't smell your own funky ass, nigger! I tell you someone's got a meth lab in these parts. I know, my jones is telling me so." Rufus breathed in deeply. "Yeah I'm smelling it now." He slowed down and opened the side window. "I suspect up that road there a spell." Both looked about the property, an abandoned tobacco farm that nature had taken over with an overgrowth of pine trees and mulberry bushes. Both spotted a chimney where smoke exhausted into the crisp afternoon autumn day, white and lazy with the still breeze.

"Let's see if we can get us some," Spike suggested.

"I don't know about that. We still have a little left over from our own stash. Plus we still got a fair distance to travel before we get to Celebration."

"Maybe we can get more and sell it down there when we get there," Spike suggested, as his voice took on an almost manic sound as if possessed by that demon deep inside.

"I suppose we could, couldn't we?" He rolled the car slowly up the road as the old house started coming into view.

A ricochet from a rifle shot and the sound of the rifle's report echoed about the trees. "They be shooting at us, Cuz!" Spike exclaimed as though he started getting second thoughts on this idea of his. "What are you doing?"

"Just hang low," he ordered as he stopped the car, placed it in park and grabbed the shotgun, leaving Spike inside. He went to a nearby tree and bounded from one bush or tree or rock to another until he somehow made it to the front door.

Spike shivered in fear as those bullets whizzed about the car, hitting it numerous times, but missing him. He felt that his bowels and bladder would release at any second as he cowered behind the front seat. Spike then peeked up to see how Rufus was doing but didn't see him.

Shots erupted from inside that old clapboard house. A moment later, Rufus came outside pushing a young girl probably no more than fourteen outside. Her fear appeared as evident as Spike's. Rufus got up to the car and put her inside next to him.

"What happened in there?" Spike asked in a halting, stuttering manner.

"Do I need to paint you a picture? I got in there and killed her pa and two brothers.

They're still inside if you want to look."

"Hey there sugar, what's your name?" Her brown eyes were big as plates. She wore a tube top over her brown skin body and a pair of tight-fitting shorts that left little to Spike's imagination. She stared at him, seemingly afraid for her life.

"Georgia," she whispered as she looked from Spike and then back to Rufus.

"I got this jones, girl. I need to get fixed up really bad, understand?"

She nodded. "I know how to do that. I seen Pa and my brothers do it all the time. Ma done left. She's over in Tallahassee partying with the college boys there."

"How old is you?"

"Eighteen," she replied. Her eyes shifted to the floorboard.

"Eighteen? Why you don't look much older than twelve!"

Rufus snorted. "Look, we ain't got all day here with a courting her. Your kin have enough mixed up to get him high and sell some when we get to our destination?"

"You ain't a real trooper?"

"Oh, hell no!" Rufus exclaimed. "I done shot one earlier and I ain't afraid of killing another either. Now answer my question!"

"Yes, sir he—Pa that is—made up a batch this morning. It should be ready by now. Can I come too?"

"Sure you can brown sugar. Georgia, that's a pretty name," Spike flirted with her. She blushed and smiled back.

Rufus pulled her out from the back seat and went to the other side where he got Spike out and uncuffed him. She led them back inside the shanty shack of one opened room and another room in the back. The kitchen was their meth lab that smelled rich with chemicals that would make anyone not familiar gag or puke.

"You go and get him fixed up while we take your brothers and Pa out back and bury them."

"Yes sir," she replied as she found her own personal stash and began getting it readied. Rufus pulled the dead father outside and Spike grabbed the heels of the two teenaged boys and followed Rufus.

After they were all three buried in a shallow grave they went back inside where the girl smiled at them with her crooked and rotted teeth.

"Here y'all are," she told them as she handed Spike the pipe worth more than gold right now for him as he snatched it from her. He lit it with a propane torch and sucked on the pipe. He inhaled deeply and his demon was satisfied. He handed the pipe back to her.

"You satisfied?" Rufus asked.

Spike smiled a goofy, aw-shucks grin that may have appeared comical in any other circumstance. "Yeah, Cuz. I be all kinds of happy now."

"Good." He turned his attention to her. "I changed my mind." No one saw him pull the holstered nine-millimeter out until three shots were fired into the girl in rapid succession. She fell in a heap upon the floor. "What the Fuck! Why'd you kill her? I wanted to party with her tonight."

"We is out of here! Get that stash and let's go!"

"But Rufus…"

Rufus' patience seemingly ran out as he placed that same pistol up alongside Spike's head. "You got a choice. Grab that stash and high tail it out of here, or you can stay here with her. Make up your mind now, Spike."

Spike saw a total stranger in front of him.

His face was now a mask of pure and unadulterated evil. He frightfully went about the place finding as much as he could grab and went outside to the trooper's car and got in. Rufus followed, setting the place ablaze as he exited that drug house and got inside the car.

"The rest of the plan remains as it is, Spike. We ditch this car and hitch a ride on the Florida side."

"How can you do this? Kill someone and act like it ain't no thing?"

"Because, Spike, it ain't nothing. We are all destined for the hereafter. It just how it goes. We was born cursed by a passion to hate. It's how I was raised and I'm sure you was raised no different.

"I hate this country, the law, those dead people in there, and I hate what I become." He shifted the car into drive and drove away from the burning shack.

At the end of the road was a mailbox, rusted with an almost bleached out name hand painted years ago: WHITE.

A MAN'S PASSION

Hattie Black walked into the museum with her great grandchild, Dot. Hattie had the features of a 100year-old woman. She was dressed in the same floral summer dress she bought in 1958 at the Woolworth Department Store in Chicago, a silver cross hung down her neck and she wore a large, brimmed hat to shade the afternoon heat.

"Grandma Hattie, tell me again how you met great Grandpa Black."

"Oh Child, are you certain you want me to conjure up that memory?" Dot nodded down at her. "Oh, very well, but let's sit here on this bench for a spell."

They sat together upon a bench, behind them were old photographs of men standing in pose in front of trees of various genus and age proudly displaying their trophies.

"Dot, you know that it's important to remember those times when I met Henry, your great-grandfather."

"Grandma, I know about history and what happened. This place is full of those times. I majored in African American Studies because of those…"

"Hush child!" Hattie scolded her. "I will tell you this story my way, or you can just forget it. Am I making myself clear?"

"Sorry, Grandma Hattie. Go ahead then."

"This story is as much about both your great-great grandfathers as anything. It's a man's passion and in that passion is always a difference of opinion. Everything in the Old South was literally black or white. You were either a Baptist, or a heathen, rich or poor, a White man, or Negro as they were called then. You were either a Southerner or a Yankee; there was nothing in between.

"Another point, young lady we were just sixty years since we lost the war of the states; Yankees called it the Civil War." Hattie watched Dot carefully, making certain she clearly understood before she continued, looking deeply into her deep brown eyes. "A man's skin color didn't mean squat, but some white men like your great-great grandfather White believed otherwise. He had opinions on everything and blamed us being poor white trash on everything except him of course.

"Child, I heard him badmouth the government, Jews and Catholics, and Negro people because it was easier, I suppose. I never paid much attention until the day of our family reunion at Uncle William's place in Polk County down in Florida. It was all two days mule and buggy ride from where we lived in Georgia on the Florida Stateline.

"I was just ten that day in 1926. We always had family reunions for as long as I can remember, but at this one I learned so much about a man's passion, plus of course I met my Henry, though I didn't know it at that time, on that day.

"I remember us riding down this old beat-up dirt road, getting beaten to death by all the ruts and potholes and noticed about a mile from Uncle William's farm was this black man heading that way too.

'Where is he going?' "Pa asked in an arrogant manner, like a Black man just walking was somehow sinful in his eyes.

"Ma told him, 'Jeremiah, let him be. He ain't doing nothin' but walkin' on this road.' "Ma was a very pretty woman. I reckoned I took most of her good looks. She had beautiful strawberry-blonde hair with the prettiest blue eyes. But don't get her riled up because those eyes took on a beastly color that scared me to death.

Anyway, she wore a breezy summer dress.

Its hem fell just above her ankles. We didn't believe in wearing those flapper dresses.

It wasn't lady-like. She wore a sunbonnet too to keep the sun out of her eyes.

"I remembered Pa and Billy wore dungarees with light cotton shirts that Ma made from the extra cotton we had from the last harvest. It was a trade of sorts, between tenant farmers. The Jones family had some cotton, we had tobacco, and another family had peanuts. It was how we survived back then. Both wore what are now called cowboy hats, though don't quite recall what we called them back then. But, like Ma's bonnet, it was the hats that kept the midday sun out of their eyes. We couldn't afford sunglasses back then."

'You stay on your side of the road boy,' "Pa told him in a menacing voice.

"I remember this Black man, he was maybe in his thirties, maybe a little older, raise his arm up in a sign of recognition and obediently moved further off the road, letting us pass."

Hattie looked at Dot. "You read books, don't you?"

"Of course, Grandma, why?"

"Ever read a book by Sherwood Anderson, called *Winesburg, Ohio?*"

"No, ma'am."

"In the beginning of the first story is about the writer who sees people as grotesques who hold on to thoughts that they gather and then call them truths, one of which is passion. Pa's passion or thought, I suppose, was that only white man had rights. He joined the KKK to defend white man's rights. It didn't matter much to him how he treated Black men.

"Passion, if used wisely, is a good thing, but Pa, his passion was sinful and hateful, as you shall see. Now back to the story. Listen carefully, child." She held Dot's naturally brown hand inside her gnarled claw, liver spotted and wrinkled.

"I once upon a time had long blonde hair that Ma braided into a pair of ponytails that fell to my back. I wore a pinafore dress that stopped just below the knees and boots that I wore all the time; school, chores, Sunday School, it didn't matter. I sometimes wore my older brother Billy's dungarees in summers when I had to help with certain chores or when we all had to harvest tobacco, but I digress.

"This morning, it was getting hot, being it was July and all. The sky was cloudless and as blue as my eyes. As I mentioned, riding that buggy on that rutted up road wore us all down and was grateful when we reached the opened gate to Uncle William's farm. I gotten good at reading and saw the sign on the post of the rail fence that read no colored people allowed."

'I wouldn't use such a nice word, myself,' "Pa informed us as we passed that sign."

'We all know what word you would have used,' "Ma told him without mirth. 'And you keep that word stuck firmly inside your mouth while we visit my brother and his family. You hear?'

'Fine, though it won't be easy. Will it Billy?'

'No sir Pa,' "Billy told everyone excitedly.

"His young mind wasn't on signs, but on the pond, he caught sight of as we turned a bend and headed up a slope. A moment later the cypress trees gave way to a wonderful white antebellum house with dog run and a cupola.

"Uncle William, something he insisted people call him, though Ma still used Billy Mack for her younger brother, owned a nice chicken farm and we all could hear a rooster crowing incessantly, while Billy and I saw hundreds of chickens scratching the ground with their growing chicks.

"Pa stopped the buggy just in front of a nice lacquer black Model T Run-about Uncle Freddy had. I spotted him holding a bat lazily over his shoulder and chewing on a toothpick. He smiled at Ma.

"Ma was the oldest of the Livingstone clan. We buried Grandpa Livingstone a year before, and he bequeathed that buggy to her. Grandpa fought for the Confederacy."

Hattie stopped and asked Dot, "Go and fetch me some water, please."

"Yes, ma'am," Dot replied. She released her hand from Hattie's and ran toward the nearest drinking fountain with complimentary plastic Solo cups. She admired the young woman Dot had become. Her slender body was dressed in tight shorts and light cotton blouse that showed her purple brassiere. When

Dot returned Hattie took the cup and greedily drank it down.

"Thank you, child," Hattie told her as she handed her the empty cup. "Be a dear and throw that away."

"I will Grandma Hattie. Tell me more of how you met Grandpa Black."

"Okay child, okay. Where was I? Oh yes. I remember. I recall how beautiful that house was. I guess it was a plantation house long ago, and Uncle William bought it when he expanded his chicken business. It kind of smelled though. Chicken poop is potent when there's hundreds of them running about. I saw an old oak tree with big, thick branches. I thought that tree was out of place. I just figured whoever owned that house long ago, planted that oak tree for a reason. I later learned that oak trees, especially that variety, are quite common in Florida. So, then I knew everything was fated to happen for a reason. God allowed that tree to grow, along with the tree that Uncle Freddie's Louisville Slugger came from. He allowed that hemp plant to grow and eventually became rope.

"Anyway, my two girl cousins came running to the buggy and Pa helped me and Ma down. He was a gentleman that way. I hugged both my cousins, and we ran toward their playhouse Uncle William built.

"Billy and Rob Roy, Uncle William's boy, a tall fifteen-year-old with a silly grin and mixing bowl haircut, ran toward the pond holding a pair of bamboo fishing poles that Rob Roy carried in his hands. Billy grabbed a pail of grubs and night crawlers.

"I heard Uncle William ribbed Pa about his beard. It was long and tangled. 'I thought you was gonna shave that thing,' he chided him.

"Like most gentlemen in the south, back then, it was more respectable to have short hair and be clean shaven. Uncle William and Freddy was no exception."

'The day we elect a Southern Democrat who believes in the superiority of the white race, I will.'

"I heard him reply with conviction. 'Woodrow Wilson was the closest, but he was more concerned with saving the world for democracy than saving the white race.'

"Both my uncles laughed at Pa, like what he was telling them was a joke. I don't think Pa was joking though. Pa had a more receptive audience back home in Georgia than here." Hattie took a breath.

"This next part is the hardest. To this day I still don't know why he came on to the property. He should have known what was going to happen if he stepped foot on Uncle William's land. Its providence is all I could figure. God wanted everything that followed to happen just as He planned. That must be it child."

A long pause followed. She looked about the museum and sighed heavily.

"Just like Jesus on Calvary, they all died for the sins of the white man."

"How can you say that?"

"It's a metaphor Dot. I don't mean any more by it. The Bible tells us Jesus gave his life so that whoever believes in Him, will never die. The same thing must be said for every black column here. Let's go find that one for Polk County, Florida."

Dot helped Hattie up and they slowly walked about each display. Some were about four or five feet tall, some shorter, and some rose almost to the top of the forty-foot ceiling.

On each column were the names etched into the stone.

As they walked, Hattie continued. "My cousins and I were playing with their dolls when we heard this commotion. I was curious and went out to see. I saw my uncles and Pa pushing and shoving that same Negro man we saw earlier on the road. Aunt Pearl tried explaining, "Bill, he comes here all the time to buy eggs."

"He can buy eggs at the colored store," Bill told her.

"I can't afford their eggs" I heard him complain. "All I got is a nickel for a dozen eggs."

"And that's all I charge him. The market charges a quarter," Pearl explained.

"Plus, mister, Otis and I don't get along!"

"Someone threw a punch. I don't know who and a melee ensued. Uncle Freddy swung his Louisville Slugger against that Negro's head with a resounding crack that sickened me. My cousins came out at that point and started crying. Pa found a rope from somewhere and threw the end over a branch of that Oak tree.

"I don't know what got over me. At first, I was crying, paralyzed in fear while I saw what my Pa and uncles were about to do. Have you ever experienced an out of body event, Dot?"

"No ma'am. Is that what happened?"

"It's the strangest thing, child. One moment I was just watching everything unfold like an idiot, then a light from God came upon me and a voice, not my own; God's perhaps? I couldn't say, resounded like a fury.

'STOP!!!'

"It was as if they were struck by a lightning bolt and a thunderclap. Everyone looked about wondering who said that, finally looking at me. I screamed at them. Remember child, back in my day no one dared tell their elders what to do; not a ten-year-old girl especially.

'You can't do this!' "I screamed at them." 'It's inhumane and immoral!'

'You best settle down,' "Pa warned me. "I wouldn't have none of that though. I knew the consequences, but didn't care if he walloped me.

"That man didn't deserve to die over a dozen eggs. I said, 'You are all sinners and if you follow through with what you're doing, murderers too just as Cain was to Abel.'

"Pa reached over to me, expecting me to cower, but I didn't. I stood my ground. He grabbed a switch and dragged me to a bench, threw me over his knee, pulled up my pinafore, baring my white cotton panties bottom and pulled them down too.

He then tried to stripe my backside with all his passion.

"Tears fell freely, and I screamed out in pain and humiliation. He finally freed my waist, and I ran away from him. I ran blindly toward the pond where my cousin and brother were fishing. Except they weren't fishing but skinny-dipping in the cool water of the pond. I stopped, curious as to why they were carrying on in that way, naked when Billy saw me and cursed, 'Dang it Hattie you weren't supposed to see this!'

"He then looked past me and yelled, "Hurry, Rob Roy, there's a lynching going on up there."

"They got dressed and ran away from the pond toward the Oak tree where that poor man hung limply."

Hattie stopped and searched for a tissue, found one in her oversized handbag and dabbed the tears from her eyes, then blew her nose.

Dot reached around her great- grandmother, hugging her close. "I can't believe they went ahead and continued to lynch that poor man, even though I told them to stop.

"It was as if their passion for what they believed in was more important than the consequences of murdering another man.

"Is this it?" Hattie asked as the column in front of them held a sign announcing Polk County Florida.

"Yes, Grandma Hattie." Twenty names were carved into the ebony granite.

Hattie saw the name and cried out, "He's there too! Artamus Lincoln Black, 1926."

Dot too became overwhelmed by the name of her great-great-grandfather shown for all to see. They held each other, their tears falling proudly down their faces, one wrinkled and white, the other smooth and mocha toned. "When did you meet Grandpa Henry Black?" Dot choked out.

It took Hattie a moment to recover, wiping her eyes and blowing her nose softly into the tissue. "That evening when his family came to take him down.

The weather had turned as if God himself was angry at the outcome; darkening clouds moved in, and wind blew in gusts as thunder rumbled and lightning flashed in the distance.

"The sheriff was there too, but Uncle William claimed he trespassed and started a fight. He was a big boned man with a Santa Claus belly. He wore a brown shirt which showed wet sweat stains around his arm pits.

He chewed on a half-smoked cigar as he heard the story William told. He displayed a big, gold star on his left breast pocket and had a revolver holstered on his right hip.

'I was defending my property,' "Uncle William proclaimed.

"Pa then piped in, 'I didn't appreciate how he was looking at my daughter and nieces. A colored man shouldn't look at white girls like that.'

'That's a lie,' "I rebutted." 'We were in Lulu's playhouse when you were pushing him about. It wasn't until after the fighting started over eggs that we came out.'

'You best keep your mouth shut young lady,' "Pa warned me.

"I remember stewing in silent rage as the sheriff continued talking with the men folk. He had a nice shiny Packard with a single red light affixed to the fender. 'So, this colored man trespassed on your property and started stealin' eggs?'

'No, Sheriff, he asked permission to buy my eggs. I told him to go and buy the eggs at the colored store.

He said he couldn't because he didn't get along with Otis, his brother,' "Uncle William explained to him.

"Pa looked distressed as if his guilt was starting to get the best of him as we all watched that man's family cut the noose from his neck and carefully laid him in the back of a mule driven buckboard. The sheriff wrote everything down on a piece of paper. Uncles William and Freddy also acted funny as they smoked cigarettes. It was as if they pleaded with their eyes the sheriff does not arrest them for what they done."

'If what you told me is correct, I guess you men were justified. Who threw the first punch?'

"All three men looked at each other before replying simultaneously, 'He did.' "They pointed at the corpse in the back of the buckboard.

'I see,' "the sheriff replied, scratching his chin in a thoughtful manner. 'I'll fill out this report and send it to the district attorney. I'll put in you felt it was justified because he threw the first punch.'

"He got inside his new patrol car and drove off the property, and your great-grandfather's family piled into the back of the buckboard, jerked the mule into action and slowly moved off the property as a deluge of rain pelted them.

"It was then I saw Henry. He talked to his brother in a low tone; too low for us to catch. They both glared at us with burning fury. I was both frightened and excited at those beautiful eyes. Don't ask me to describe any more Dot. It just gives me nightmares every time I think about it. I don't think my old heart could handle that.

"The very moment I saw his eyes blazing with fury like they were, I fell in love with him and knew he was mine for the rest of our lives. "Naturally, I made an excuse to go into the house but asked Cousin Lulu where his kin folk lived. She laughed, thinking I was kidding with her until she saw how serious I was.

'Hattie, why did you ask such a fool question?' "She asked me with amazement.

'I want to pay my respects and apologize for my family's ignorance.'

'What? We done nothin wrong. That colored man trespassed. Pa has every right to do what he done.'

'You gonna tell me or not?'

'They live outside Celebration. I don't want to play with you no more. You got something wrong with your head. Ma warned me about you before you arrived. Now I know why.'

"I ignored my cousin. She never changed; still insisted the confederate flag be flown outside her house until the day she passed. She was proud of her bigotry, she was."

"Why did you go see him?" Dot asked.

"To exchange addresses. What shocked me though was the next morning. You see I planned to sneak out the next morning, borrowing my brother's trousers, shirt and hat so I would conceal myself as a boy. I was surprised to see my uncle sitting inside the dog run smoking a cigarette. But I'm getting ahead of myself here.

"That night as I laid awake in bed, I had hundreds of thoughts running through my head like a flooded creek. The rain outside didn't help. I could hear it striking the windowpane and the rain gutter outside.

"I prayed and prayed. It seemed like it took all my energy to ask the Lord's forgiveness. I didn't know how God was gonna punish my uncles and Pa. I didn't want to see them end up in hell for all of eternity, but Pa's passion infected my uncles in such a way that it was like a dry rot that caused them to hang that poor Black man.

"I couldn't imagine my uncles also carried the same passion. I refused to believe it. It ain't their nature. Ma told that to me and Billy hundreds of times whenever she overheard Pa describe a Black man in some odious and hateful way.

'That ain't how my brothers treated them colored folk,' "she'd reprimanded Pa repeatedly.

"You see child, I was in turmoil all that night. I long ago believed with all my heart in my Christian faith and nothing was gonna change, especially a passion for hate that Pa carried like a bag of luggage.

"Back then it was acceptable behavior, and regular Christian folk like Ma and me felt like outsiders. I had hopes that one day this day would finally come. This place is like a tonic for those of us living with the guilt we carried all these years. I am now truly proud to be a southerner. Dot, now I can go to heaven free of guilt for the first time in 90 years."

"What happened between you and your Uncle William?"

"Oh yes, Uncle William. He was 100 years old when he passed away in 1989. He saw so much change that I couldn't begin to imagine what he must have thought before that day the Lord finally called him Home. My time is drawing near too. My Henry is waiting for me. But I digress.

"Uncle William was hidden in the shadows of darkness inside that dog run."

'Where are you going?' "He asked me, nearly scaring the life out of me. I think I remembered screaming, but I quickly recovered."

'I have something I need to do,' "I told Uncle William."

'You know, I feel bad about that. I shouldn't feel pressed to act the way I did. You are right child; it is immoral and sinful. I don't think Jesus will ever forgive me. I know I should have stopped your pa.'

"He took a long drag from that cigarette, as if he was considering something. I wanted to tell him not to fret since I was up all night praying for Jesus' forgiveness.

'I should have stopped him. I'm not like that; like your pa, I mean. I think the only reason my sister married him was to get him to change. I should have told her; there's no changing a man whose passion is hate.'

"He finished his cigarette and grounded the butt in a silver-colored tin ashtray."

"How you'd know it was silver colored? It was dark, weren't it?"

"Dot, I saw that ashtray in broad daylight the day before. Now stop interrupting me. Now, where was I? Oh, yes, now I remember. I saw a tear roll down his cheek in the gray predawn light. I wanted to cry too, but instead, I turned to go opening the screen door and fixing to leave.

'Wait, I got to drive to the colored market and unload a crate of eggs. I'll take you to his place.'

"Uncle William pulled himself from a rocking chair he had and went with me outside. 'How you know?' "I asked suspiciously."

'I saw how you looked at young Henry. It's the same look my wife gave me before we started courting twenty years ago. You are infatuated. Don't worry, your secret is safe with me. Help me load those eggs.'

"I followed him to the barn where he stored the big Dodge delivery truck and just nearby, were a crate of eggs waiting to be loaded. The barn smelled of old manure, hay bales and chicken feed. It also had a slight pungent odor of gasoline and oil from that truck parked inside.

That crate looked heavy, and I wondered if maybe Rob Roy shouldn't be out here helping too. But Uncle William was a big strapping man in his younger days, unlike Pa who was a bit soft and lazy.

"I did no more than watch him hoist that crate up from the ground and set it on the truck bed. All I did was direct him to where the bed was and get out of his way.

"I opened the garage door. It wasn't like they have now, rolling up on a cord and rollers. It was a pair of doors that swung out. Once he pulled the truck outside, I closed the door for him and got myself inside.

"I never rode in a car before. Sitting in that shiny red truck, all polished and pretty, made me feel so proud. Unlike the rutted-out road Pa took, Uncle

William took a right turn as soon as he got off the property and was on a smooth paved road that led us toward the town of Celebration.

"Uncle William cleared his throat, as if he was fixing to tell me something."

'Like I told you before, it ain't my nature to do what I allowed to happen yesterday. I knew him. His name was Artemus, though everyone knew him as Art. The reason he and Otis didn't get along was he caught his brother stealing food. Otis would have gladly given him food to feed his children, but Art had other plans for that food. To this day I don't know what Art's motive was and it saddens me to think how cowardly he must be to steal from his own brother like that.'

"I stared at him. I'm sure I gave him some quizzical expression because I weren't certain what he was trying to tell me that could possibly justify lynching that man yesterday. I saw the sun rise on my right and the rain clouds we experienced the night before had moved north of us, possibly into Georgia and Alabama.

'Are you suggesting you were justified in what you did because of a theft of food?'

"I asked him like I was a Sunday School teacher or a church deacon. Yup, I was feeling even more disappointed by his excuse than by Pa's insistence on lynching him. The reason made no sense at all.

"As far as I was concerned, Uncle William should have just told me he did it to teach Artemus Black a lesson.

"Uncle William nodded slowly. I could see smoke rising from a burn pit where the colored people burned their refuge. I remember it stunk.

'Uncle William, can I be honest with you? "I asked him. I figured he knew what I was gonna say but nodded anyway.

'Your idea of an excuse stinks as foul as that burn pit yonder over there. If you didn't trust Artemus, why did Pearl allow him on the property to buy your eggs?'

'She didn't know. I never told her about him stealing that food.'

"I remember rolling my eyes at him. 'You should have told her. She would never allow him to step foot had she known, Uncle William.'

"I stared out the truck's window. All kinds of feelings jumbled inside. At that moment I loved and hated all adults. They made my world more complicated than it deserved. My thoughts were in a whirl. Why did he do that? Why didn't he tell Aunt Pearl? I was heartbreak sick over this episode."

"What did he do then?" Dot asked. "He apologized. I saw the hurt and shame in his gray eyes. He looked as if he had aged ten years; guilt ridden that he was."

'I promise it won't happen again,' "he told me, and I believed him. I smiled at him and wanted to hug him, but the gear shifter was in the way, and it probably wasn't becoming while he was driving toward the colored market. I stifled the urge until we finished our business.

"We stopped at the edge of town and came upon the colored folk neighborhood. It wasn't much; a bunch of rickety-looking houses, dirt yards and down the dirt road was the colored market, and next to that was the Calvary Baptist Church. I think I remembered seeing a couple fields with stalks of corn and other vegetables growing there too."

'Morning, Sir,' "I heard a deep baritone voice boom behind me, and I saw it was the storekeeper who greeted Uncle William with a bashful smile and offering his hand. Uncle William shook it."

'I'm terribly sorry what happened yesterday, Otis.'

'I'm sure you are, sir. As it was, my brother and I weren't close, Mr. Livingstone, or I would be telling you all where to take those eggs. As it is, I reckon he trespassed on your property, and you felt justified by your actions.'

"He scared me because everything he said was in a quiet, respectful tone, and it was said with such intelligence, Dot."

'You got the crate I ordered?'

'It's in the back. Oh, this is my niece, Hattie. She wants to visit Henry. Hattie, this is Henry's Uncle Otis.'

"I looked at the big man who hid the sun so well. If I thought Uncle William was big, he paled in comparison after seeing Otis Black. His big hand covered mine and I feared he could easily crush it if he wished.

"Instead, though, his hand felt-feather soft. He smiled down at me, and he had the same beautiful eyes as Henry. His black hair was kinky and short, with slight traces of gray appearing along the edges."

'My, you are a big man,' "I exclaimed in awe.

"He gave me an awe-shuck smile and blushed. I remembered laughing at him."

'We buried him last night, and in about an hour we are going to do a sendoff,' "Otis told us. 'You all are welcome to come join us.'

'That would be just fine,' "Uncle William said respectfully.

"I remember they both worked together unloading that flatbed truck of the eggs and then Uncle William helped him set up a display to help sell the eggs faster, though I reckon that wasn't necessary here. Back in them days, everyone ate eggs.

"Well, before we knew it, people from all around this little neighborhood started packing that little church. It wasn't much to look at; like all churches it had a simple steeple with a white cross on top and a high-pitched roof. There were windows that brought in the natural sunlight.

"Suddenly, the place came alive with songs and hand clapping. I had to go in and see for myself.

"Lord, it was a remarkable sight. All of them, women, children and men come together to praise Jesus and send their dearly left on his way.

"I felt the power of the Holy Spirit, Dot. I began clapping in time and rhythm to the gospel songs they were singing, and tears of joy fell down my face. Then Uncle William joined me. He too appeared overwhelmed by it all.

"The preacher started preaching and the singing slowly receded, though they continued clapping their hands and crying out hallelujahs and praise the lords throughout his sermon. During all of this I spotted Henry and slowly made my way to him.

"He acted scared of me and retreated. But then his hard eyes softened, and he seemed to know what brought us together and accepted it.

"I slipped him a brief note that also had my address. The note said I'm sorry about your pa and want to be your friend. We can write like we were pen pals if that's okay, Hattie.

"He read the note and nodded. I remembered Uncle William pulling me away. I noticed some of those Black people looked at both of us with quizzical expressions.

"I think William was afraid there might be a confrontation if we stayed longer. I suppose upon hindsight his guilt was starting to get the best of him.

"There now child, that's the story, except for what all happened later. Tarnation, I'm thirsty. Go and fetch me some more water, Dot."

Henry, we got us one beautiful great granddaughter. She's smart as a whip too. I think she's gonna change the world for the better. I just wish I could live to see it all unfold. I guess I'll just have to see it all in spirit, like you have all these years since you gave your life. Did I do good raising your children by myself? I hope I did.

"Yes, Grandma Hattie," Dot replied nodding at her with those same soft brown eyes her Henry had.

When Dot returned with another cup of water, Hattie continued, "On the way to Uncle William's place, I went to ask him a favor."

'What is that, Hattie?' "Uncle William asked me as he kept his eyes on the road in front of us."

'Cut down that oak tree and make me a four-poster canopy bed from it.'

'I can do that.'

'Also, whatever is left, make a casket for Pa. I want him to rest in peace, knowing the tree he lynched a man on, is his eternal home.'

'You know, I recollect having a dream like this, Hattie. I'm gonna make you a cane too. There will come a time in your old age when you must revisit everything that happened. You'll need a cane to get around.'

"I nodded agreeably-like as we continued to his place. Just then we both spotted the sheriff coming to us from our side mirrors. His single red light was flashing, and he turned his headlights on and off, forcing Uncle William to pull over and stop.

"The sheriff came out of his car, pulling his ten-gallon hat up over his flaming head of red hair. I swear girl, I never saw a man with such red hair in my life.

"Anyway, he stepped up on the running board on Uncle William's side and says, 'How do, Mr. Livingstone.'

'How do, Sheriff. What do I owe this unexpected pleasure?'

'Coroner came back with the autopsy results. It showed he died from strangulation due to a rope being tied about his throat. It seems he suffered considerable because it was a slow way of dying, Mr. Livingstone.

'I must ask, why didn't one of you all put him out of his misery? A bullet ain't but a nickel a piece.'

'I was so perplexed by the whole episode; I weren't thinking straight. It wasn't my idea to hang Mr. Black in the first place, but her Pa, Jeremiah White.'

"He spied on me as if for the first time and at once apologized. 'Oh, forgive me I thought that it was Rob

Roy with you. "I remembered smiling across at him His face got as red as his hair from the embarrassment.

'It's quite alright,' "I quipped. I let out a grin that I'm sure looked perfectly evil because it took him a moment longer to recover."

'Anyway, me and the district attorney are gonna ruled this homicide, justifiable because of Mr. Black's criminal history and you being an upstanding citizen of Polk County and all. Have a good day sir, young lady.' "He quickly stepped away from the running board and Uncle William shifted gears back to first, released the clutch and continued back to the farm.

"An hour later, he had a chainsaw he brought out from the tool barn, and he proceeded to cut that tree down. I thanked him and I thanked God in a silent prayer."

Dot looked at her great grandmother with as many conflicting thoughts and emotions as Hattie had when she was that ten-year-old girl 90 years before.

"You are right Grandma Hattie; it was a very different time than what we have now. What happened to Aunt Pearl and Grandma Ruby?"

"Well, child, they both lived to be old and died a few years ago; Pearl died before Uncle William back in 1980 and Ma passed in 1979. They also experienced a lot of change, as I have. You showed me a lot of these past three days. I think it's time we pick up stakes and head back to that 'assisted living facility.'" She used her two fingers off each hand for quote marks.

"Where you want to spend the night?"

You know, I ain't been to Tallahassee since I graduated in 1936. I surely would enjoy seeing how much that place has changed."

Dot thought a moment about that. "It's gonna be a long drive from here to there. We might need to stop overnight again."

"That's quite all right child. I was expecting to anyway."

"We'll take the same route back to Columbus, then go south to Tallahassee," Dot told her as she navigated the Google map on her cell phone."

"Child, that's fine."

"Let's go then." They both left the museum with the same slow, purposeful gait as when they arrived. The cane and their shoes echoed off the polished cement floor. A white man pushed a trash can by them. He smiled at them as he stopped to empty a trash bin, heaping full of paper cups and plastic straws. "Grandma, I'm starting to feel a bit hungry. Would you like to stop and eat somewhere before we hit the highway?"

"That would be a fine idea, Dot. I think some of that Popeyes Chicken would sound good right now."

"I thought you didn't eat no fried food, Grandma."

"I don't eat it all the time; just on occasion."

"Well, the other night…"

"I wasn't hungry for fried chicken the other night. Now, I am."

"You amaze me sometimes Grandma."

"I'm just trying to keep you thinking. Ain't nothing wrong with that."

Dot could only nod at Hattie's logic as she maneuvered to the car parked in the halffull parking lot. More cars came in, just as a few other cars left.

Two hours later, they were back on the highway. Dot drove the Prius with a full belly. Hattie fell asleep, snoring while Dot maneuvered over the divided highway. Steady traffic flowed at 70 miles per hour.

Hattie stirred just as they both saw the same abandoned truck, right near the exit they needed to take south toward Tallahassee. "That's a bit odd," Hattie said.

Dot nodded, took the exit, and then made a left, going over the overpass to the other side of the highway. She merged with the traffic flow and fell in behind the truck. Hattie caught her breath, startling Dot. "What's wrong?"

"Over there on the side of the road by that truck. I think there's a body over there."

"Dear Lord, stay put Grandma, I'll be right back." Dot placed the cell phone in her ear after quickly dialing 9-1-1.

"Hello, I've come upon something on the side of US 280. I think there might be a body on the side of the road. It's near an abandoned truck.

"My great grandmother and I saw that same truck yesterday and a trooper was parked behind it. Should I get out of the car and see who it is?"

"Don't be getting out of this car young lady," Hattie ordered her.

Dot ignored her and walked toward the truck and went to the side where she too saw the same dark lump. She stopped in her tracks, still talking on the phone to the emergency dispatch center. She did an about-face and walked back toward her car when a trooper's cruiser pulled up. His overhead lights were on, and he parked behind Dot's.

"Show me your hands!" the trooper yelled at her.

"I'm talking on the phone," Dot replied, figuring he could tell who she was talking to.

"I said show me your hands, now!" The trooper was white and a little older looking than Dot. He also looked scared as he reached for his Glock 13. Dot raised her hands.

"There! You satisfied?"

He went to her and grabbed the phone from her, spun her around and placed cuffs on her.

"Wha…I was calling 9-1-1!"

"Yeah, well we'll see," he replied. He escorted her into the back seat of his Charger.

Hattie opened her door and slowly made her way out of the car. She finally pulled herself up using her cane. Her legs shook with effort.

"Young man, why are you arresting my great granddaughter?" Her voice didn't carry well with the traffic flowing on the highway.

Four more Georgia State Patrol cars arrived. All were Chargers and all four troopers were white. They ignored Hattie and ran to the area where Hattie told Dot a body might be. Hattie watched their reaction.

One vomited, one called on his portable radio, "10-43 Murder Reported, trooper down; code name Mike-Uniform-Romeo-Delta-Oscar-Charlie-Kilo. Copy?"

"Copy, 14:45." The female dispatcher replied. "I will alert CSI and State Forensics."

Hattie saw the other two troopers quickly retreat to their vehicles and started working at securing the crime scene. They taped off a zone that included Dot's car, the abandoned truck that they suspected was stolen and a pair of Georgia White Pine trees they secured the tape to.

She then slowly, purposefully, walked toward the first trooper who came on the scene. Dot fumed inside the trooper's car.

"Young man, I want to talk to you!"

"Who are you?" he asked in a startled tone, as if he hadn't noticed her before that moment.

"I am her great grandmother, young man," Hattie pointed at Dot with her cane.

"Why in tarnation did you arrest her?"

"This is an ongoing investigation, ma'am. You shouldn't be here. Do you know someone who can pick you up?"

"What kind of foolish question is that? Young man, that girl sitting in the back seat of your patrol car is the person who brought me here in the first place."

He gave her a look that told Hattie he was either extremely confused or the biggest moron she'd ever come across. "You witnessed him getting shot?"

"NO!" Hattie's fury saw no bounds. "My great granddaughter did not shoot him. We saw the abandoned truck with two young men standing outside and a trooper just pulled up. That was yesterday! Do I need to draw you a picture?"

"No ma'am," he replied but still acted confused. "Why are you here?"

"Oh, my word. Young man we just finished going to the lynching museum in Montgomery and we were headed back to my nursing home in Coral Gables, when we both spotted that same truck still parked there. We both thought it peculiar because we figured the truck broke down and that trooper come to help them poor black men out."

For the first time the trooper showed a sign of clarity as his face brightened up.

"But the trooper's car is gone."

"Well, I guess those men that were here, must've taken it after they shot that trooper then."

"Yes ma'am," he replied and ran to the other troopers. "Hey, it wasn't that girl after all." He yelled after them. "The grandmother told me what she thinks happened."

"Really, Olsen? And what did she say?"

"That they just come back from Montgomery and saw that truck yesterday with Trooper Murdock pulling them over. It seemed to her that there might have been a breakdown, and he had come to help. She seems to think two Black men who were with this truck must've shot him and escaped using our patrol vehicle."

"So, the girl ain't a suspect after all?"

"No sir. Should I release her?"

"That would be a clever idea. I want statements from both those two."

"Yes sir," Trooper Olsen replied as he went back to this Dodge cruiser and let Dot out from the passenger seat and uncuffed her.

"I'm so sorry for the misunderstanding, ma'am."

"It was because I'm Black, wasn't it?"

"Ma'am?"

"You thought I killed that trooper because I am Black, and you all profiled me as a suspect. I should sue the Georgia State Patrol over this one."

"I…I just assumed…"

"Young man don't ever put forth a fool's notion like that. It gets you in nothing but trouble," Hattie scolded the young trooper.

He tipped the brim of his hat and retreated from the pair.

Eventually, the incident commander arrived and ordered the crime scene tape removed from the Prius. He was a bear of a man with large biceps that threatened to tear the short sleeves from his shirt. He wore captain's bars on each collar and his barrel chest threatened to pop the buttons off his shirt. He walked up to the pair of women and removed his hat to them.

"I am terribly sorry for t h i s misunderstanding," he told them in a sincere apology. "I hope you would see it in your Christian hearts to forgive the Georgia State Patrol for what happened."

"I'll consider it sir," Dot told the trooper. "Are we free to leave?"

"Yes ma'am. Can you give us all your names? I want to send you a gift for our sincere apology to this unfortunate incident."

"I'm Dorothy Mae Black and this is my great-grandmother, Hattie Black. I live at the campus of Georgia Tech, and she lives at Mannford Manor Retirement Community at Coral Gables, Florida."

"I promise to make good on this. Again, my humblest apologies for what happened," he said as he wrote the information in his black notebook.

Dot helped Hattie back in their car, and they drove back down the highway until they caught sight of the nearest overpass to exit and go back east to the South US 27. Dot set the cruise control at 65 miles per hour. "Grandma, I was curious. When you all rode that buggy down to Florida from Georgia, where you all spend the night? There weren't many motels back then, was there?"

"Oh Dot, Dot, Dot, you are so naïve, it's humorous. We camped wherever we could along the way every night. We were dirt poor tenant farmers. It took all the little savings from the previous year's tobacco crop to afford to take that trip.

"Whenever we stopped for the night, Billy handled taking care of Milly our mule, I had to gather wood for the cook stove we brought. It ain't what you think.

Pa saw this camping stove in the Sears and Roebuck catalogue. He also bought our first outhouse with it too. Anyway, Pa set up a lean-to and Ma cooked the vittles. It wasn't much; beans, cornbread and jerky. Then, once it got dark enough, Ma and I would sleep in the buggy, while Pa and Billy slept on the ground."

"I guess us taking this road trip is a bit of a luxury compared to how you went down to Celebration and back, huh Grandma?"

"Well, naturally it is much preferable for this old body. It wasn't too bad sleeping on that leather seat cushion; right comfortable actually, except for the bugs and mosquitoes."

The drive proved a bit uneventful, though long and they did have to stay overnight at a motel in a small Georgia town.

The next morning, they reached the Georgia-Florida state line. Hattie spotted the trooper vehicle before Dot, though she quickly tapped her brake to cancel the cruise control. Once they drove past, both noticed the car was empty. "That is a bit curious, Dot."

"Should we call someone?"

"I don't know. I hate to have another repeat of what happened up in Columbus."

Dot nodded and pressed the resume button on her steering wheel. The car quickly went back to 65 miles per hour.

Five miles further down the road, they spotted two Black men walking along the highway hitch-hiking for a ride.

Normally, Dot never bothered, yet she felt they needed her help and pulled over 50 yards away. They ran up to the car.

Hattie recognized the two from two days prior. "Those two were the ones stopped by that State trooper near Columbus the other day, Dot."

"Are you sure?"

"Pretty much, Dot."

It didn't take long for Dot to put two and two together. She pressed 9-1-1 and waited for the dispatcher to come on.

"911, what is your emergency?"

"I'm on Highway 27, be quiet for a spell. You are on speaker." She watched the pair come up to her car and unlocked the back doors for them.

"Oh, hey there you two. Where you headin'?"

"Celebration," replied a big, powerful man that Dot figured was in his early to mid-thirties. "I got me some cousins who live there. This is my bro, Rufus. I'm Silas Lee Black, but my friends call me Spike, on account of that director. You know Spike Lee?"

"Oh yes, I'm Dorothy Mae Black, but my family calls me Dot, and this here is Great grandma Hattie Black. She lived in Celebration for a spell, didn't you Grandma?"

"I surely did, Dot. We are only going as far as Tallahassee. I'm going to see the Florida State campus one last time before I see my final reward; seeing my Henry, where we'll live in the presence of our Lord and Savior for all eternity."

"She's gonna be 100 next week. We just came from the Peace and Justice memorial up in Montgomery," Dot informed the two passengers.

She looked up in her rearview mirror to see her new passengers. She glanced at the cellphone and saw the low battery sign come up. Her hopes dashed instantly.

"Grandma, it sure is curious about that patrol car just up the highway like that, just on the other side of the Georgia state line. Did you boys see that too?"

"No ma'am we didn't come across no abandoned car," Spike replied quickly.

Hattie felt the urge and told Dot, "Child I need to visit a powder room somewhere, right soon."

"I think we need to keep going," Rufus replied in a not too subtle threat.

"I'm sorry, but I made that mistake three days ago. I just now got the stink out," Dot told the two. "There's a rest stop up the highway. I'll just stop there for a minute."

"You'll do no such thing," Rufus told her as he pulled the dead trooper's Glock 13 and held it to her head. "You just keep driving until I tell you to stop."

"Where you get that gun from?" Dot asked as she too felt the urge to release.

"Oh Lord, don't do nothing to my great-granddaughter!" Hattie screamed.

"You just shut your mouth old woman, or you won't live to see the sunset," Rufus threatened.

Hattie released the fecal matter into her adult diaper. "I hope you all are satisfied."

"Oh my God! Grandma Hattie!"

"What the hell is that smell?" Spike asked with disdain.

"I warned you all. She needed to go," Dot explained.

"Stop the car!" Rufus yelled at them. As soon as Dot pulled over, he ordered them out of the car.

"One of you all is gonna have to help me out," Hattie told the two men.

"Spike help her out. I wanna have me some of this sweet brown sugar. You can have that old bag of bones. You said yourself you like white meat."

Spike ignored his comment as he escorted the elderly woman from the car.

"I'm truly sorry for this, ma'am."

"I'm a bit curious young man because I used to live in Celebration for a spell. You got kin there?"

"I have some cousins who still live there. My great grandfather lived there until he was shot by a sheriff in 1960."

"Did he ever mention about his brother?"

"Not in so many words he didn't. Grandpa had nothing good to say about his uncle though. He called him all kinds of names."

"You shut the hell up, Spike. I don't to want to hear your stupid family yarns again. Who cares if your great-great gramps got lynched? It didn't change how you become. "You admitted yourself he was a thief, just like you become; a part of the family tradition," Rufus exclaimed to his partner.

"I remember that day," Hattie told them. She also saw the flashing red and blue lights of many police cruisers heading in their direction. "Dot did I ever tell you what they taught us the other day at the nursing home?"

Dot could only shake her head in terror, while Rufus held the gun to her head with his right hand and fondled her bra enclosed breast with the other. Sweat fell from her brow, combining with the tears that fell down her cheeks. She breathed rapidly.

"This," Hattie replied as she thrust the cane into Spike's groin, garnering a deep breath intake. Hattie then threw the cane straight up into Spike's nose. Blood gushed in all directions.

Finally, she swung her oak cane against the side of his head, and he fell to the ground, gasping for air. He stopped breathing. "Sorry Spike."

"You a crazy and stupid bitch. Now you both is gonna die."

"You ain't gonna shoot us," Hattie said with confidence.

"Drop the gun, you stupid fucking son of a bitch," yelled a Florida state trooper, his face a mask of fear and heightened adrenaline as he placed a bead of his service revolver, a Glock 37 on Rufus's head; the only clear shot he had.

"Go to hell," Rufus replied before turning the Glock on the trooper. A deafening explosion and a crimson hole occurred simultaneously on Rufus' forehead.

Dot screamed. The stolen Glock discharged but missed the Florida trooper by inches. Rufus fell in a heap to the highway's pavement. Blood poured out.

Hattie smiled. She then fell to the ground, lying next to Spike, her great-great great nephew, and exhaled her last breath.

"Grandma, no!" Dot raced to Hattie's side and tried to hold her up in her arms. She felt remarkably light. "Don't go now Grandma!" Tears of sorrow replaced tears of terror, and she cried over Hattie's still form. "Don't go now."

2045

Dot sat on a rocker at the annual Black family reunion surrounded by her adult grandchildren and holding a newly born great granddaughter. They were in a garden surrounded by lilies and roses. The lawn green and lush and the May sky as blue as Grandma Hattie's eyes. Dot's hair had turned white with age; facial lines deep on her forehead, mouth and eyes. Sitting next to the rocker was Great grandma Hattie's oak cane, smooth and varnished with a deep brown hue. Dot's right hand rested on the cane's crook.

Young Hattie Mae sat next to her grandmother. She had her great-great grandmother's looks, though her skin tone was just a shade lighter than Dot's, with the same blue eyes. She'd just turned nineteen the other day.

"Grandma, tell us again about how Great great grandma Hattie saved your life, please."

"Oh, child, you don't want me retelling that yarn again."

"Sure, we do. Come on Grandma, tell us."

"Oh, okay. I first must remind you about a man's passion. You see passion can take many forms, hate, lust, greed. In this case it was a passion for life; to carry on the family name so that all of you would be here today. All those things make our lives what it is; a man's passion."

End

www.ingramcontent.com/pod-product-compliance
Lightning Source LLC
Chambersburg PA
CBHW031553310726
48973CB00003B/806